CONTEMPORARY AMERICAN FICTION

SAY GOODBYE TO SAM

Michael J. Arlen's books include *Exiles* (nominated for a National Book Award), *Passage to Ararat* (winner of a National Book Award), and three collections of essays on television: *Living-Room War*, *The View from Highway 1*, and *The Camera Age*.

SAY GOODBYE TO SAM

Michael J. Arlen

PENGUIN BOOKS

PENGUIN BOOKS
Viking Penguin Inc., 40 West 23rd Street,
New York, New York 10010, U.S.A.
Penguin Books Ltd, Harmondsworth,
Middlesex, England
Penguin Books Australia Ltd, Ringwood,
Victoria, Australia
Penguin Books Canada Limited, 2801 John Street,
Markham, Ontario, Canada L3R 1B4
Penguin Books (N.Z.) Ltd, 182–190 Wairau Road,
Auckland 10, New Zealand

First published in the United States of America by
Farrar, Straus & Giroux Inc. 1984
Published in Penguin Books 1985

LIBRARY OF CONGRESS CATALOGING IN PUBLICATION DATA
Arlen, Michael J.
Say goodbye to Sam.
(Contemporary American fiction)
I. Title. II. Series:
Penguin contemporary American fiction series.
PS3551.R4447S2 1985 813'.54 85-9536
ISBN 0 14 00.8224 7

Printed in the United States of America by
R. R. Donnelley & Sons Company, Harrisonburg, Virginia
Set in Janson

This book is for Jennifer, Caroline, Elizabeth, and Sally Arlen and for Robert, Patrick, and Alicia Hoge

SAY GOODBYE TO SAM

What I remember about that spring in the city is how the wind used to blow at night, a real wind too, like in the country, bending the spindly little trees and making the old windows rattle. And then it stopped. For a while it seemed as if there was no weather. I couldn't sleep and so I'd wake up early, an hour before dawn sometimes, and sit at the table in our kitchen—the round formica table—looking out across the rooftops and down at the empty streets. There was such stillness everywhere, like a great peace, like death too. Then around six o'clock I'd go back to bed where Catherine was still asleep, on her side, one arm outside the covers, legs bent like a kid, and lie close to her, listening to her breathe, waiting for the sun to rise and the day to start and the empty streets to fill.

I didn't tell Catherine about my early-morning vigils though once she woke up early too and came into the kitchen where I was sitting. I think I said I was trying to figure things out about my work, which was also true. I'd turned thirty-nine some months before and found much to think about: not maudlin philosophic thoughts about age or being nearly forty, because I rather liked being older; there was something about it that seemed almost like a promotion, like finally making officer's rank. Unlike many of my friends I was glad at last to be a grownup, and so fretted over grownup matters: careers and real estate and suchlike: whether to expand my last magazine piece into another book; whether to put aside trying to write decent journalism ("serious nonfiction") and take an editor's job if it was offered to me; whether to spend the money my mother had left me on a larger, more uptown apartment, and so on. I thought about but never worried over Catherine. It was her great gift to me, I felt, more precious than her youth and beauty; I mean her steadiness, her healthy normalcy, the quality she had (I think one could call it this) of simply being there.

That spring we were not quite two years married and already I'd virtually forgotten Tessa: her preppy cuteness and sad infidelities and endless tantrums—our six years of wedded shipwreck. Catherine was thirty in March; not old, not spoiled or silly young, though young enough to think of me as a somewhat older man. A New York girl she looked like at first glance: dark hair, dark eyes, that confident, professional way of gazing out at the world. She was professional too, worked in the design department of a publishing house—a rising star a friend in the department said, though Catherine herself seemed to have no interest in rising further and talked instead of turning freelance or even staying home for a while. Of course, like most New York girls she came from somewhere else; in her case a white-collar suburb about an hour from Cleveland. Just an average place she used to say. An apparently happy, uneventful childhood. But both her parents had died when she was twenty-two, and though there was a dour, crew-cutted brother who sold computer peripherals somewhere in Florida I always thought of her as an only child, like me.

An only child, a lonely child. I don't know when I began to think that Catherine was lonely. Perhaps that talk of "staying home." Perhaps a look she'd sometimes get in her eyes, late in the evening or Sunday afternoon, of someone traveling too light, of someone whose life had been stripped too clear of family. In some ways I suppose the two of us were bound together, even brought together, by a shared imprint of loneliness, although I didn't understand that then. I thought I had handled my mother's death pretty well. I thought Catherine was the best thing that had ever happened to me. I thought I'd be strong for both of us.

And what I also thought one day in spring, three years ago, is that it would make her happy to see Santa Ana that summer. If she was lonely I would give her that final part of me, the only part I had left to give: the ranch at Santa Ana. Not exactly the place I'd grown up, for I'd grown up in too many places—both coasts as they say; too many hotels and rented houses and boarding schools. Still, if it was something less than home, less than ancestral roots, it was more than most other sites and situations: the focus of our family life I guess you'd call it, in the years when my mother and father were still married, and when we still had (in a manner of speaking) a family life.

My father's ranch. Where my father still lived. I thought I'd give Catherine *it* and *him*, at least for a few weeks in the summer. I thought I'd be strong enough to make him like me.

So did I suddenly sniff the dust of the Southwest one morning in the smoggy city winds? No, I never did that. But I remember when the idea of the thing appeared aloud, slipped out into sentences one morning, a Saturday morning in late May I think it was. Our bedroom warm with sunlight. The big quilt half off the bed. Two coffee mugs and part of a newspaper on the floor. Catherine moving around the room, barefoot, half naked in pale blue underpants, her hair wet like a swimmer's from the shower. The walls are chalky white in need of painting. The windows open wide, letting in the usual sounds: traffic, kids playing down the block. "I think we should go out to Santa Ana in July," I said.

She was standing across the room from me, holding one of the little three-dollar plants she'd buy at the market and tend as if they were pets. At first she didn't say anything, as though she hadn't heard me. But then, very quietly, she said: "You want to see your father?"

"I want you to see my father," I said. I wondered

if she could see inside my head and knew what I was thinking. The fact is I wasn't thinking anything just then. I never thought about my father. Never saw him, talked to him, dreamed about him. We didn't, as they say, communicate.

Catherine was bent over the little plant, smooth white legs, bare feet on the straw rug. It passed through my mind that in some way I was thanking her for all those times she hadn't asked me, hadn't pushed me, hadn't poked me with a stick like Tessa and all the others. "How can it be that you don't ever *see* him?" they'd say, each one so eager to meet, to be charmed by, to make the acquaintance of my famous father. But how could I explain that he and I were merely an accident of kinship? That he'd passed through my life like a night rider, a highwayman, and that the sum-total of his regard for me, and eventually of mine for him, was zero. Catherine was standing upright now, a yellow plastic watering pitcher in her hand. "I'd like that," she said. And, "It's what you want, isn't it?" And I said, "Yes," because, whatever happened, I'd have her with me.

I said I never thought about my father but the truth is for long periods of my life I couldn't remember anything about him, except I suppose for his being tall, and for the oddest details—details of dress they often were: a certain kind of hat he wore; a gold money clip someone had given him, shaped like a dollar sign; a blue silk scarf he used to drape around his neck—not so much around his neck as across his shoulders. The scarf I think was a present to him from my mother the winter we were in Rome together, back in the early fifties, "not long after the war," as people dated time in those days. We stayed in that huge gray hotel just off the square (at least it seemed huge to me at eleven): dark marble lobby and ancient threadbare armchairs and men in greatcoats walking in from the cold wet streets outside. I think he'd just finished directing a movie in England (*Flight to Tempelhof*, it must have been) and was now in Rome having talks with some Italian producers—about which project or projects I don't know, for in the end I don't believe anything came of it. This was in the heyday of his "international period," when he was forever taking ships or planes to distant parts, making pictures as he called them, or making deals about making pictures, while my mother and I (on leave from school, or simply "between schools") dutifully trailed after him. I know I wanted to like Rome. My mother certainly wanted me to like it. "It's going to be such a treat for you," she said in her enthusiastic voice before we left, doubtless hoping it would turn out that way for her as well. And, "Imagine going to Rome at your age!" Years later when I went back there as an adult, as a magazine correspondent in another winter, I was struck by how the pink and amber buildings glowed with light and warmth, how the sunlight sparkled everywhere. But that winter long ago I remember no light, no warmth, no sun, no glowing pink or amber. Instead drear skies; wet sidewalks; cold floors; cold sheets in bed at night—enough to chill the marrow as my mother used to say.

We had a number of rooms in the huge gray hotel: a suite I guess it was, with a fancy bedroom and living-room arrangement for them, and a small adjoining room for me, and then a room nearby for prim Miss Ferguson, who handled correspondence and appointments for my father when he was abroad, and under duress helped my mother with her clothes and errands, and even took some vague supervisory charge of me when they were out. My recollection is that they were nearly always out (though rarely out together), and

I was always in, lying on my bed trying to keep my attention on a book (my mother was keen that I not "fall behind" in my reading), or trying to persuade Miss Ferguson to play gin rummy, or wandering downstairs to hang around the lobby and spy on the somber men in military uniforms who often sat about the bar, sipping drinks in exotic colors and eating fistfuls of nuts. But then there was no telling when my mother might return; usually late in the afternoon when it was already dark, but sometimes early, after lunch, around two or so, rushing into my room, hugging me fiercely, with a kind of distracted crossness ("Look at you! You haven't even been *out* today!"), and then *out* we'd go, in a taxi, or now and then in my father's hired Citroën if it was available, honking our way through the rainy streets to some gloomy museum or damp church, or once into the incomprehensible immensity of St. Peter's. "I know you'll tell your children about this someday," she said to me afterward as we were sitting in an indoor café having hot chocolate for me, vermouth for her, and little cakes for both of us. She had a way of eating her cake with her fingers, like a child, and then looking back over her shoulder as if someone were about to come in and tell her not to.

I didn't see much at all of my father in Rome that winter, but then I never did. "He's a very busy man," my mother used to tell me, though whether explaining his absences to me or to herself I didn't know. I already knew he was a very busy man. In fact, I seldom minded his being busy; I felt there was a sort of stability, an order to things, when he was elsewhere, working. One day she told me that he and I were going to "do something together"; he was going to take me out to one of the big studios on the outskirts of the city to watch the filming of one of those big costume epics—*Hercules* or *Son of Hercules* or some such thing. I was instructed to get properly dressed. And to be waiting in my room. And not to be late. "Now don't go wandering about," she said. "I won't," I said. In due course the hour for the great expedition came, and (as I knew it would) went. So did another thirty minutes; another hour. My mother herself was off somewhere. I found Miss Ferguson drinking tea in her room. "He's probably delayed in traffic," she said and patted me on the head, the first time she'd ever done a thing like that. I waited out a full two hours and then went downstairs to the lobby. For a change it was a nice day outside. The big fortress-like doors, normally closed against the rain and cold, were open wide; a uniformed porter was kneeling on the marble floor polishing brass. I followed my usual route, loitered near the newspaper stand, sat for a while in one of the tall chairs facing the front desk, then wandered off to the right in the direction of the bar. It must have been mid-afternoon. The cavernous dining room was empty, with one or two waiters clearing up after lunch. In the musty writing room an old lady was seated at one of the desks writing post-cards. Inside the bar—a long rectangular room with heavy green curtains and hunting prints on the walls —there were four people seated around a low table at the far end: three men and a woman: two men in raincoats so it looked like, a woman in a dark suit, and my father. I felt I should probably leave; back off as quietly as I'd come in. But I didn't. One of the other men was talking. I could hear my father's voice breaking in—low, harsh, jocular. He was making a joke of some kind. The others were laughing. And then he saw me. His eyes staring at me across the floor. His face suddenly like stone. I thought: I turn his face to stone. He had the blue scarf draped around his shoulders. He beckoned me forward and motioned me to an empty chair between the two men in raincoats. One of them was talking about someone called Simon who had either just made or lost a lot of money. My father told a story about Simon that again made everybody laugh. The waiter brought me a Coca-Cola. One of the men produced a briefcase filled with papers, laid the papers out on the table. The woman asked me if I enjoyed school. At one point my father said, "The trouble with Leo is he thinks you can rent the fucking Sahara." I don't know if he said anything at all to me or not, or if he even looked at me, but I know how strangely safe it felt to be in that chair, in that harsh dangerous place, with him nearby. And then he looked at his watch and stood up. "Christ, I've got to go," he said. For a moment I thought he was about to take me out to watch the movie being filmed, but then he looked down at us, the other men and me, the papers on the table, and said, "I'll see you guys." And turned and left the room, the woman following behind him.

There's another afternoon in Rome that also sticks with me. Late afternoon. A pale gray light everywhere. I'm in my room. A book and playing cards on the bed. My mother and father are both off somewhere. I think they may even have gone out together this time. The hotel is very quiet. Outside the windows, the city itself feels silent, as if asleep. Then I hear voices on the other side of my door, *their* voices, coming from the living room. Muted at first as if they're talking quietly, whispering, exchanging secrets. But there's an odd rhythm to the dialogue. Unmistakable inflections. A new and frightening kind of music. My father's voice is deep as usual, but has a surprising flatness to it. My mother hisses, quick, jagged sounds, sibilant, like a bird, her voice rising, rising . . . Then there's a crash! Like an explosion; like destruction. And silence. The noise was so loud I think a window must have been broken. Many windows. But the hotel—everything; everywhere—is suddenly as quiet as before. I'm standing in the middle of my room. No, near the door. My hand is on the doorknob, turning it . . . Inside the next room I see my mother standing alone, her back to me. Fragments of a glass vase lie on the carpet. A small pool of water. A dozen or so long orange flowers are scattered at her feet; gladiolas they must have been. "I had an accident with the flowers," she said. I started to pick up the pieces of broken glass. "Watch out, don't cut yourself," she said. I wondered where my father had gone and what had happened; there was something about the light in the room that made it seem as if he'd never been there. I picked up the flowers and gave them to her. She was standing in the middle of the room, holding the orange gladiolas in her arms; then she shook her long hair from side to side the way she sometimes did when she was trying to make up her mind about something, and said, "We better find some water for these, shouldn't we?" Years later when she was living in that little house in Baltimore, not long before she died, I talked with her about that winter in Rome, but of course she remembered it all quite differently. "I guess we had our fights," she said, "but I know we never smashed a vase. I know we never *broke* anything." And, "Will you ever forget St. Peter's and that golden winter light? Wasn't it all so thrilling?" But when I saw those orange flowers on the floor, I think what I knew was that one day he and she were going to break up, and that he was going to leave us, and I suppose by the same token we were going to leave him.

We were driving across the desert when the storm hit. Great black clouds floating in, solemn and heavy, across the mountains to the west. You could almost feel the wind come up, see the dust swirling above the sandy flats. We'd been steaming along the new highway, air conditioner revved up to max, the radio crackling with country chatter: New Mexico crop reports and livestock news. Catherine was over at the far end of the seat, notebook on her lap, felt-tip pen between her lips. She brought a little spiral notebook with her whenever we took a serious trip (two such trips in two years of marriage) and entered, as far as I could tell, anything from occasional private thoughts to details of scenery and even weather. It was a habit I guessed she'd picked up when traveling with her parents and not yet abandoned. "Is there any music?" she said. Her voice so even, level, calm. I loved her matter-of-factness, her simplicity. I loved *her*. Pretty face in profile. Legs stretched out straight toward the floorboard. Long legs in tan cord trousers. There was an evening before we were married, driving in this same car into the New England countryside. The Stockbridge Inn was where we were going; a weekend in early fall. Catherine wore a dress that time; a kind of light madras skirt that rode far up her legs, her thighs. I wondered, did she know it had ridden up so far? Had she meant it to? That evening I'd put my hand on her leg, her bare leg, and moved it up and up and finally under her skirt. Such a sweet feeling: that nest of softness under my hand. Now, another time and place, I saw again her long, limber legs and wished them bare of corduroys and whatever else. I reached to turn the radio off. My hand on the knob. At which point there was a loud burst, almost an explosion, of static and noise, and then the rain hit the windshield.

For the first few seconds I literally couldn't see the road. A frightening moment with our car sailing down the highway at 70 mph and a sluice of water pouring down the glass in front of me as if we'd just submerged. I started the wipers vainly wiping, also slowed the car down, also turned off the damn radio. The road ahead looked like a river, dark and slick. It felt as if we were moving through a tunnel of rain, ourselves still strangely dry but surrounded on all sides by a world of storm. Bright bolts of lightning close by the mountains. Rain everywhere. Drumming, smacking on the roof like pellets. Black clouds low overhead. I decided to do the sensible thing: pull off the road and wait for the torrent to pass over us.

"Why are we stopping?" Catherine asked.

"Because it's safer," I said.

Once I remember we were flying in a small plane, one of those little commuter jobs, coming back from visiting friends on Cape Cod. Thunderclouds all over the sky on our way down to New York. You could see the lightning flashing out of them in the distance. Then nearer, a mile or so away. Then less than a mile. "Are you frightened?" I said. "No, I'm not frightened," she said. The anvil clouds were all around us. You could actually smell the electricity in the cabin. At one point the plane dropped suddenly and she leaned over and kissed me on the cheek. "I'm not worried because you're going to take care of me," she said.

Now we sat together in the car, dry and safe, but also in some way exposed, like troops caught out beyond their lines in a bombardment. What you could see of the afternoon sky outside was dark and purple, as if the clouds had been steadily draining the light from the wild yellow landscape. I thought of turning on the light inside the car but decided against it. The engine was still running to support the air conditioner; I switched both off.

"I like the rain," Catherine said, and rolled down her window a few inches.

"You'll get soaked," I said.

"I don't mind," she said.

Almost unbelievably, the storm seemed to increase. It was like being beaten down, pounded.

"It's so hot in here," Catherine said. Her hair and face were wet and dripping from the rain that poured in through the slice of open window, but instead of moving away she rolled the window down still more until she could stick her head out.

"Catherine," I said, wanting to tell her I loved her, wanting to tell her something. I wanted to tell her we were caught way beyond our lines—were miles and miles from home.

She pulled her head back in, rain-soaked and glistening. Rubbed her cheeks. Started to roll up the window.

"Come nearer," I said.

She looked at me; dark eyes cool and serious.

"I couldn't hear you," she said.

I put my hand on the back of her head, against her hair, meaning to do I don't know what: touch her wet hair, squeeze the water from it. The raindrops rattled on the car roof. I leaned forward, kissed her cheek, her mouth. Kissed her mouth again. I could feel her body tense against me.

"Tom?" she said.

I stroked her breast through the outside of her shirt, then put my hand underneath it.

"Please don't, Tom," she said. She was pushing against me with her hands.

"It'll be all right," I said. Two claps of thunder very loud outside the window. I had my hand between her legs.

"No," she said.

My hand against the rough fork in the corduroys.

"No!" she said. And, "What's come over you?"

"Yes," I said. I meant please. I meant everything would be all right. I started to undo her trousers.

"No, Tom!" she said, pressing at me with her fists. And then, almost shouting in my ear: "All right, I'll do it! I'll do it!"

She rolled away from me on the seat and in the same motion unclasped her trousers and pulled them down her legs. "What now?" she said. Angry, confused.

"Just lie down," I said. And so I fumbled with my own clothing. We were all legs and feet and trousers, cold bodies together, with the rain coming in through the window above our heads. Myself inside her. Not dry, thank God. Not wet. Not good. Not sweet. Not all right.

She was silent afterward, putting on her cords.

"It's never been like that with us before, has it?" she said, staring out the window at the nearing mountains, for the storm had passed and we were back to driving. I wanted to explain to her what had happened but I didn't know what had happened. After a while she reached down beside her feet and picked up the soggy remnants of her spiral notebook. "Look, it's ruined," she said, but not really to me, and without rancor. "I'm so sorry," I said. "So sorry." And God knows I was.

Red rocks. Green dots of juniper on the red hillsides. The sky milky and clearing as we came into the valley. "Breathe the air!" my mother used to say as we reached the high country. Puffing on her cigarette. Charlie Converse at the wheel of the Land Rover: our hand, our cowboy, our foreman as he preferred to be called, though we were in no need of foremen. Clean-shaven for the occasion, grinning, chewing on his Skoal. My friend and hero. "Ain't you two a sight for sore eyes," he always said meeting us at the airport, then a half day's drive away. Once there was still snow on the mountains. Once coming through the foothills we saw two eagles high above the valley, wheeling, circling, drifting with the currents. "Breathe the air," I said to Catherine, and without looking at me she rolled the window down again and took my hand.

It seemed just typical of my father that he'd be out when we arrived. "Something probably came up," said Catherine. "It doesn't mean a thing." We were both milling around in the big room just off the entryway: a large old-fashioned ranch living room cluttered with animal skins and Indian rugs and pottery and beat-up leather furniture. I alternately strode about, secretly surprised how little changed everything appeared to be (even the dust on the windows looked the same), or sat down here and there trying to act composed.

"He told you he was going to be busy," Catherine said.

"He could have been here," I said.

"Tom, don't look for trouble," she said.

I could see her point, could tell that once again I was dangerously close to making a fool of myself where he was concerned. I also knew in my heart that I was right; that it wasn't some unavoidable emergency or press of business that had caused my father not to be there. He always managed *not* to be there, to be somewhere else when you needed him. Not truly absent, let it be said, but operating according to a sense of time or place that seemed deliberately designed to unsettle anyone who might be waiting for him.

Catherine was wandering around looking at the rugs and pots. "This is a lovely room," she said.

"It could do with a cleaning every ten years," I said.

"Oh, Tom," she said. But I could feel her mood had lightened. She was happier than when we'd arrived, drifting across the floor like a dancer. "It's just like I thought it would be," she said. "Those beautiful old rugs. Do you see that red-and-brown one there. The red's so bright, like—"

"Like fire, isn't it?" my father said behind us.

We both turned around and there he was, striding in from the bright light of the outdoors, moving across the room, by God tall as ever, big, unmistakable in rumpled black trousers and work shirt and square-toed boots. I stuck my hand out to greet him; that's how we always did it: a handshake. His hand felt hard and heavy. "How do, Tom," he said. He smiled at Catherine. "Hello, I'm Sam Avery," he said. "I'm pleased you're here, Catherine." He shook her hand too. "That's a nice little rug, isn't it?" he said, looking in the direction of the red-and-brown rug she'd been admiring. "Fella in a three-piece suit came here all the way from a museum in Texas, wanted to take it back and examine it with some electronic gizmo. I had to tell him the Indians made it without e-lectricity and I didn't see how e-lectricity was gonna improve it any now."

"It's beautiful," Catherine said. "Everything's beautiful here."

"God's country," he said. "It's probably why he leaves half the state like such a junkyard. You know, I was just riding up in the hills and found a mess of old tin cans that must have been laying there for forty years. I'm telling you, you drop something around here and it stays dropped till Armageddon."

"You're looking pretty good," I said. It was no less than the truth. The old man looked damn good. Old, yes. In a way I was rather relieved to see that he finally looked old. There'd been a time about ten years ago when he was actually in his early sixties but looked much younger; looked permanently stuck in middle age, as if he was refusing to surrender any more of himself to Father Time. But now his hair was white, and sparser on top. His creases etched more visibly. His eyes were no less bright but set deeper into parchment cheeks.

"If you want to know," he said, turning to Catherine, "I think I look like a very old archangel. Keep in mind of course that Lucifer himself was one of the archangels."

"I'll keep it in mind," she said. "Do you ride every day?"

"Most every day," he said. "A little saunter up in the hills. Gets the blood moving." Suddenly he seemed restless, maybe noticing our suitcases for the first time.

"Didn't you go up to your room yet?" he said to me sternly.

"Which room?" I said.

"What do you mean *which* room?" he said. "The upstairs room."

"There are several rooms upstairs, aren't there?" I said.

"The *guest* room," he said as if speaking to a child. "The room at the end of the corridor."

"It sounds lovely," Catherine said.

"Damn right it's lovely," he said. "Maria! Maria!"

A woman appeared from one of the several doorways to the right.

"Goddamit, Maria, where have you been?" he said.

At first glance she was dark like an Indian but without either roundness or softness of face. Black hair, black eyebrows. Sharp strong features as if chiseled out of wood. It was hard to tell if she was young or old; I guessed about forty. She stood a few feet away from us, hands folded in front of her cotton smock.

"Maria, we're going to put my son and his wife in the upstairs guest room," he said.

"Okay," Maria said, not moving.

"I'll go get the bags," I said.

We had three suitcases in the hallway: one for me and two for Catherine. I started to pick up one of Catherine's, and my father seized the other two.

"Come on, I can carry something," Catherine said.

"Nonsense," my father said, heading up the stairs.

"Here, let me take one of them," I said, trying to

lay a hand on my suitcase. After all, it *was* mine and he was seventy-two.

He turned on me, eyes ablaze. "Goddamit, if I wanted help I'd ask for it!" he said. We proceeded up the stairs in silence: my father, Catherine, and I following Maria to the second-floor landing, then down the long corridor to the room at the end.

"Oh, it's wonderful," Catherine said.

Indeed it was. A fine room: spacious, simple, a plain wood floor, a nice bed, a dresser, table, two chairs, a fireplace in the corner. Maria hoisted one of Catherine's suitcases onto the bed.

"Please don't bother with that," Catherine said.

My father was surveying the scene, hands on hips. "*This* is the upstairs guest room," he said dryly.

"It's very nice," I said.

"Does the fireplace work?" Catherine said.

"Fireplace doesn't work," he said. "Fireplace is kaput. Squirrels put junk in there all winter long." He scratched his belly and hitched up his trousers. "Well, I've got things to do," he said, looking at me as if I'd just asked him to read a Babar book aloud to us.

"Sure," I said.

"This is a damn busy time," he said, still staring at me.

"We won't get in the way," Catherine said.

He smiled at her. "I'm sure you won't, my dear." Then, "Maria, we'll leave these young people for a while." But Maria had already left. "We have dinner early out here in the country," he said to us. "We'll meet around seven-thirty. Nothing fancy." He paused in the doorway as if he was about to say something more, but then he just turned and left.

After he was gone I walked over to the window. Far away in the distance, the blue mountains ranged across the horizon at the far end of the valley. They had a proper name of course: Sierra Nocturna, Mountains of the Night. But for me they were always the blue mountains, remote and magisterial in the haze. Down below, no more than thirty yards away, the little creek flowed by, over white and yellow stones. Willows on the bank. The same old cottonwood, its right side blackened by lightning.

Catherine was resting on the bed.

"What do you think?" I said.

"I love it," she said. "It's so sunlit and simple. Basic, like real country."

"I mean about him," I said.

"He's pretty basic too," she said with a laugh. "I think he's great." She looked so young just then, lying on that bed—a girl in shirt and corduroys, clear-eyed, smooth-cheeked: a face that had most of its seasons and marks ahead of it. I wanted us to forget what had happened earlier in the car. I wanted us to stay safe together like children in that room.

Dinnertime, that first evening. My father stands at the sideboard in the dining room, tugging the corks out of a couple of bottles of red wine. There are five of us around the table: Catherine and me, showered and dressed in our Nothing Fancy clothes; also the Bonaventuras—"the neighbors," as my father describes them: George and Priscilla Bonaventura, who have a ranch about a dozen miles away. He's very much a Westerner despite his name—short and stocky, with a tough, good-humored face and a fringe of steel-gray hair around his head. He's probably in his early sixties. His wife is younger, early fifties perhaps, and has an Eastern, vaguely aristocratic look about her—a handsome woman with long straw-colored hair, a large silver bracelet on her wrist, a string of pale purple jewels around her slender neck. And then there's Trent. His full name is Harrison Trent but I've never heard him called anything but Trent. Years ago he was my father's assistant on *Cardoza Is Dead* and I guess he's worked on and off for him ever since. When Trent is around, it usually means a deal is cooking, a project is about to materialize. He must be fifty now himself, a little heavier in the chest and gut, but with the same unlined, impassive face.

My father pours from one of the bottles, moving around the table where we're seated, managing to be both shambly and ceremonious at the same time. The wine is ruby red—caught in the flicker of candlelight—and somehow beautiful. The old room itself just then is beautiful: white walls; dark wood on the floor; the Spanish table and sideboard; the silvery glitter of the candleholders; another splendid rug hanging on the far wall.

Priscilla Bonaventura picks up one of the bottles and examines the label. "Goodness, Sam," she says in her New England voice, "this is very first-rate."

"Damn right it's first-rate," he says. "We got first-rate company, don't we?" He sits down in his chair at the head of the table, clumsily, happily, like a boy sitting down to a long-awaited meal, in this case a mess of cold ham and red beans. "Maria!" he calls loudly. Maria appears from out of the kitchen, wearing a little faded green apron over her dark smock. "Is there plenty of that hot sauce in these beans?" She stands behind him, holding a bottle of what must be hot chili sauce, and puts it down on the table in front of my father, who doesn't even nod in her direction but takes the stopper from the bottle and pours half its contents on the beans on his plate, then stirs them about, brings a forkful to his mouth, smacks his lips, swallows, roars with delight. "By damn that's good stuff," he says.

"Sam, I don't see why you bother drinking good wine if you splash that filthy green sauce on everything you eat," Priscilla says.

My father winks broadly at the rest of us and continues shoveling down the beans. "Never drank wine until the war," he says between swallows. "That's a fact. Used to drink beer when I was young. They had some mighty good beer in Chicago. German stuff from Milwaukee. Then whiskey when I started work. Rye whiskey was what I used to drink before I knew better. It had that funny taste so you'd sweeten it up with a little soda pop. I remember a *Herald Tribune* guy called Dunning, Tony Dunning, who used to drink it but without the soda pop. 'Only pansies and out-of-towners put soda pop in it,' he told me once. Christ, he was from farther out-of-town than I was. He was from your state, George."

"Idaho?" says George.

"Nah, Dunning was from Montana," my father says. "Hell, I thought you were from there too."

Maria comes out with a large plastic bowl filled with leaves of iceberg lettuce and pieces of carrot, covered with a thick orange dressing, and bangs it down in the middle of the table. My father is temporarily silent at his end, thinking, dreaming, who knows what. His face looks weather-beaten and leathery in the dim light, like an ancient desert animal.

"What happened in the war to get you drinking wine?" I hear myself say.

He looks up quickly. "Who the hell cares?" he says.

"Don't be such an old grouch," Priscilla says, patting him on the arm in a familiar way. "Come on, tell us."

He takes another drink from his glass, wipes his lips. "My son here wants to know what his daddy did in the war," he says with his gambler's grin. "Ain't that sweet? Fact is I didn't do shit. I made a documentary about Third Army that nobody saw, and I helped liberate Château Belleville."

"From the Germans?" Catherine says.

"Hell no, sweetie," he says. "The Germans were long gone. From Georgie Patton. We were attached to Third Army but running along with the Fourteenth Division. There was Bobby Harding from Movietone, and a guy called Demarest from *Colliers*, and Larry Middleton from *Life*. God knows what we were all doing besides wasting the taxpayers' money, but as somebody said it was a hell of a war if you didn't have to fight it. We had these two Jeeps and a couple of drivers from Special Services and when the Fourteenth turned south we went south too. I think Demarest had a girl in Cannes from before the war, or thought he had a girl in Cannes. Christ, everyone had a girl in Cannes before the war. Anyway, we got ourselves lost, and somehow got out ahead of the Fourteenth, and there was this big old house in the middle of a vineyard. Château Belleville. Women and old men still working the place. Cases of stuff piled in the cellar. Well, we all knew General Patton's fondness for the finer things in life, and figured he'd probably cart the whole damn château back to Virginia or wherever he lived if he found out about it. So we put a sign outside. A sheet it was, hanging from the front gate: 'Off Limits to U.S. Army Personnel.' In due course they sent a captain down from headquarters to find out what the hell was going on. Larry Middleton met him at the door and hustled him right back outside. 'Typhus,' he explained. 'They're trying to keep it quiet.' So we just stayed there the rest of the week, drinking our way through their great prewar vintages, watching some muddy little river down below, trying not to think about the war . . ."

"Did you finish yet?" Maria says, standing beside him, reaching for his plate.

"No, I did not finish," my father says. "Can't you see? Does it look like I've finished?"

"If you speak all the time, how can you eat?" Maria says.

After she vanishes with the rest of the dishes my father announces in a conspiratorial whisper, "I try to let her think she bosses me around."

Tell me, are you a lot like him?" Priscilla said.

"I'm nothing like him," I said.

"*Nothing?*" she said.

"We're opposites," I said. "It's kind of a genetic marvel."

"You mean, you're the quiet one?" she said.

"I'm the quiet one," I said.

"You don't tell war stories?"

"I don't tell war stories," I said. "Actually I don't tell any stories. I don't remember any stories."

"But you're both creative," she said.

"No, *he's* creative," I said. "I'm a journalist. *Je suis journaliste.*"

"You don't make things up?"

"I try not to make things up."

"Well, you still look a lot like him," she said.

"I know," I said. "I think it confuses the hell out of both of us sometimes."

Trent in his leather airman's jacket disappearing down the corridor after dinner. "He's so quiet," my mother used to say. "You never know he's around until you see him, and you never know he's left until you don't." There was the time we lived in Santa Barbara; not for very long, maybe one fall. A big white house with a tile roof. A lawn like a golf course. A fig tree near the driveway. A swimming pool always filled with leaves. My father was making a movie at one of the studios. *Nogales*, I think it was, with Reynaldo Forbes. The way things worked, my mother and I lived in the house in Santa Barbara and he stayed at a hotel in Beverly Hills and came out on weekends. "He's really terribly busy," she'd say, and, "He's under so much pressure," this being in the days when she still felt nice about him. Also, "It's better for your schooling." I was ten and was briefly enrolled in Santa Barbara Day School, the most unashamedly comfortable school I've been to in my life. Real silverware at lunch. Blue cloth napkins. All those rich California gentry kids with their little crested blazers and chauffeurs. Tony Vlassos drove for my father and sometimes drove me to school. But he wasn't a chauffeur, my mother explained, he was a driver; there was a difference. If Tony was big and Greek, thick hands, hard, friendly face, then Trent was something else. Cool, austere, unflappable. It seems to me he even wore a leather jacket back then, but it couldn't have been an airman's jacket since only airmen wore them in those days. "What does Trent *do*?" I asked my mother. "He takes care of things," she said. A man of many lists and few words. I remember sometimes he and Tony Vlassos would play cards together in the little room just off the kitchen, waiting for my father to go back to town. Neither of them talking. Tony and his bottle of beer. Trent and his cigarettes. For a while I thought Trent took care of actual *things*—flat tires, leaky faucets—and maybe he did that too. But then I realized what he mostly took care of were problems that other people didn't want to bother with, or perhaps touch. Smoothing things out with the cops on location. Dealing with the Teamster drivers. Getting my father clean shirts. Keeping my father's mistress Esther Tobey out of sight. Fixing my mother's parking tickets. "Always leave it to Trent," I can hear her saying cheerily, the two of us together in that white house. "Trent can fix anything!" I think it was maybe the only part she liked about my father being famous, or maybe it was the only part she liked about that long summery autumn in Santa Barbara: that Trent could take care of parking tickets for her.

With everyone else finally gone, my father and Catherine and I were still sitting outside on the porch, looking out at the night and the stars. The old man kept clearing his throat as if he were about to say something of significance, but then I realized he was just clearing his throat. I wanted him to ask me about my life; my work; to say he'd read one of my books; to tell me he was glad to see me. But I knew as usual I was going to ask *him*.

"Are you planning a new movie?" I said.

"Yes, what are you working on now, Mr. Avery?" Catherine said.

"What's this 'Mr. Avery' crap?" he said to her with a friendly growl. "*Sam*, for chrissakes." He took a swig from his brandy glass. "Fact is, I'm working on something damn good. Could be big, very big."

"I just knew it!" Catherine said.

"You knew it?" he said. "The kid must be psychic. Let's see if you know what it's about."

"I don't know that," she said.

"Guess," my father said.

"I can't," she said.

"Come on, you have to guess," he said.

"No," she said.

"Guess!" he said.

"I *can't*!" she said, her face suddenly tight, frightened, like a child who's been pushed too far. "Please don't tease," she said, looking away from him.

"I wouldn't dream of teasing you, Catherine," he said with surprising gentleness.

She looked up shyly. "It's something about out here? The mountains and desert?"

"Close," he said, puffing his cigar. "Maybe close enough to win the jackpot. Fact is, we're talking about Arizona, a border town, so it's more desert than mountains. But desert is right on the money. We got a bang-up story. All the right elements."

"What elements?" Catherine said. Oh, literal Catherine! Should I have warned her against provoking the wolf with too much literalness, too many questions?

But the wolf was wearing grandmother's cap. "You want me to list the elements?" he said.

"Yes," said Catherine.

"Well, first we got an old Ambrose Bierce story," he said. "Public domain, thank God. We update it a little. Instead of an army deserter we have a terrorist on the run. We got suspense. Is he gonna get away? Who's gonna get to him first? We got romance. There's this girl from one of those right-wing families who wants to go with him. We got beautiful country, but nobody gives a damn about beautiful country except you and me. Did I say politics?"

"No," said Catherine.

"We don't have too much politics because you drive 'em out of the theater with politics. But we get in some good stuff. What makes these terrorist guys tick. What happens to revolutionary movements when they get out of control. Important stuff." He leaned back, pleased with himself. "I'm telling you it's the real McCoy, ladies and gentlemen."

"It sounds wonderful," Catherine said.

"We're calling it *Rio Rigo*," he said. "Working title. Has punch."

"Don't you think it sounds great, Tom?" Catherine said.

I felt his eyes on me. "Tom is thinking," he said. "Tom is mulling over his opinion."

"It sounds terrific," I said. "Who's the terrorist running from?"

"Who the fuck do you think he's running from?" he said. "He's running from the government and he's running from his own guys. I told you that. He's a deserter."

"When do you start?" Catherine said.

"Screenplay's finished," he said, "but needs a little work. Refinements. Polishing. An abundance of riches you might say. We're in the process of closing the deal."

"Who's the writer?" I said.

"A very talented young fella," he said. "Doesn't run with either the New York or Hollywood crowd."

"Saul Bellow?" I said.

"Very funny," he said. "Very funny. The boy's a humorist. The writer's name is Donald Newcome.

He's coming down next week. They know all about him at CBS and NBC, but he's too good for TV."

"A television writer?" Catherine said.

"You have to learn the technique somewhere," my father said.

"Oh, I agree," Catherine said. "Besides, they have some very good things on TV."

"They have shit," he said. "But let me tell you something, a lot of these young guys are way ahead of where we were—way, way ahead."

"Oh, I think it's so exciting," Catherine said, looking at me, then him again, her eyes so happy; in fact, I wondered for a moment which one of us had come home.

There was a photograph in a silver frame my mother used to keep around when she was married to him. My father in his younger days. A lanky young man in shirt-sleeves, suspenders holding up his trousers, hands in pockets, standing outdoors in the sunlight in front of what looks like a stone farmhouse, half grinning, half squinting into the sun—his quintessential fuck-you look. I think the farmhouse was somewhere in central Mexico and he was down there shooting *Cardoza*: his first big movie, *Cardoza Is Dead*. It's a good movie too. They teach it in film schools and you can still catch it sometimes on television as part of Public TV's Screen Classics series, along with *The Grapes of Wrath* and *The Maltese Whatsis*.

I remember reading somewhere that he'd been a "boy wonder" in the movie business but the truth is he didn't even start in the movie business. He spent an unlikely year at the University of Southern Illinois in the early thirties, vaguely majoring in geology.

Then quit to work as a sports reporter for the Springfield paper. Then left Springfield for Mexico and a job with the *Chicago Daily News*. I've sometimes heard him say, "When I went to Mexico for the *Daily News* . . ." which suggests he was dispatched to Mexico City the way CBS sent Ed Murrow to London. What I think happened is he went to Mexico that first time on his own, and found a revolution going on right under his nose, and somehow talked his way onto the *Daily News* as a stringer. The Cárdenas revolution is what it was, and I guess he must have covered it pretty well. Bumped a lot of European stories off the front page back in Chicago. Made a small name for himself as a correspondent. The *Daily News* brought him back to the foreign desk but he didn't stay. Then someone at MGM asked him to rewrite an already much rewritten foreign-correspondent screenplay about to go into production: *Easy Winners*. Not exactly a Screen Classic (though Trevor Dunn looks impressive in his trench coat), but it earned some money for the studio and so they hired him—a contract writer in their screenplay factory.

He was supposed to be an amazingly fast worker. I once read about him writing an entire screenplay over a weekend and I don't doubt it; he had a sure, quick eye for scenes, and if the dialogue was sometimes a little obvious it certainly had force—or, his word, punch. Also, I have the feeling he wasn't too weighed down by concerns of authorship; he'd take other people's stuff and recycle it, his own stuff and recycle it; the point was to keep moving, keep working. It's hard for me to picture him in those days. Young and ambitious and good-looking and doubtless a bit awkward. But always confident. A fast learner. A savvy young guy from the Midwest. In books about Hollywood there are any number of references to his films, but strangely enough very few to him personally. Occasionally he'll crop up at a Garden of Allah party with the East Coast literati. There's a story about him playing polo with Darryl Zanuck and Averell Harriman. A hoary anecdote about a drunken caper with David Niven and Johnny Grahame. But mostly he seems to have gone his own way, a crowd unto himself. "I've always been a very lucky guy," I remember him saying long ago to a roomful of people, and I think it's probably true. Come to think of it, it was luck of a sort that brought him and my mother together. "The only time I took the Broadway Limited instead of the Century, and there was Laura, the best-looking woman in the club car," is something else I heard him say in better times. Or maybe I read that too.

The luck he had in Hollywood was this. The director of a film he was working on came down with mumps a few days before shooting was scheduled to start. There was talk of delaying the project until the director could get back on his feet, but my father apparently persuaded a key figure at the studio, J. B. Floraman, first of the frightful contagiousness of the dread disease, then of his own ability to do the job. I guess you could say that once my father sat himself down in the director's chair he never got out of it. The movie was *Incident at Three Rivers*, loosely, very loosely based on the old story of Chief Joseph and the flight of the Nez Percé Indians, and it became a solid hit. A crowd-pleaser and a critical success, largely because of the old man's then original idea of making a heroic figure out of the Indian chief. He did two other pictures very rapidly after *Three Rivers: Hannegan's Heroes* and *Fort Kearny*. Not great, but good solid action stuff. Like most of his films, mainly stories of rebels and rebellion: guys talking back, hitting back, and shooting back at other guys, with some roughneck, wise-guy fun, and not a little plain meanness thrown in to keep things moving right along. And then *Cardoza*.

Cardoza put him on the map, the big map. Lifted him above the two dozen or so American directors who could do decent, popular work, and put him up there for a while—in fact for a long time—with the select few who put their special stamp on films. Of course, having Gable helped. And Reynaldo Forbes as Colonel Cardoza. And a luscious girl they found in Mexico—Silvia Riva—who just dropped from sight afterward. What I think lasts best about *Cardoza* is its energy. Scenes as crisp and tight as the best Hitchcock or Ford. Others with that pell-mell flow of incident you associate with the most modern school. And always running underneath it—a track beneath the sound track—that strangely innocent go-fuck-yourself quality he always managed to work into his best movies. He got a wonderful performance out of

Gable; the only time he's ever looked dangerous on screen, as opposed to that Rhett Butler manly-swagger kind of thing. And there's a scene near the end that can still make you sit up after all these years: the famous train chase where Gable is being hunted through this crowded, ramshackle, refugee train by Ernst Lukas as the sinister Ramírez. A lot of people think *Cardoza* won the Oscar, but it didn't. "Hollywood politics," my mother said, which I think was another way of saying that Academy voters preferred movie musicals that year. In fact, the old man didn't win his Award until ten years later with *Dakar*, one of those big-money, big-screen pictures he started making in the late fifties and which no one shows much anymore, not even on late-night television. I remember the year he won we were living in Connecticut, though I was away at boarding school at the time. The headmaster called me into his office one morning, very solemn and stiff behind his desk. "I suppose you know your father won the Academy Award," he said.

"Oh yes," I said, for some reason adding, "He wrote me about it." This was a lie on several counts. I hadn't known and he never wrote me about anything.

"But I thought it was announced only last night," he said.

"He wrote me that it was going to be announced," I said.

The headmaster kept looking at me across his desk, pressing his fingertips together in a headmasterly way.

"Well, you must be very proud," he said at last. "Of course I don't see many films myself, but I hear it's very enjoyable."

"It's the best movie ever made," I said with sudden abandon, for the truth is, no matter how much he let me down, I always thought he was terrific when it came to making movies.

It felt awfully early when I heard Catherine's feet moving across the bedroom floor and the sound of the bathroom door being opened and shut. My watch said seven-thirty. "What's going on?" I said as she started to get dressed.

"I heard him up a while ago," she said.

"He always gets up early," I said. "It doesn't mean you have to get up too." I probably should have warned Catherine of my father's mania for early rising. I've never known a man so chronically incapable of staying in bed in the morning. Always up with the rooster, puttering around, working, not working, arranging, rearranging. But what would I have said? That no matter how early you get up the old man will always be up before you? Catherine tugged at her pretty hair with a hairbrush, preparing to descend into the wide-awake world. "Honest Injun," I assured her from the bedclothes. "Don't worry about when he gets up. It's not a competition."

"Do you want some coffee?" she said.

"At seven-thirty?" I said. I didn't mean to be difficult but I've never liked early mornings in the country, all that empty time and space waiting to be filled.

By eight-thirty I was more awake, though no coffee had yet appeared. I tried sulking for a while, marooned amid the sheets. Perhaps Catherine was only being sensitive to my need for sleep! More likely she was off on one of her walks, exploring the terrain. I got up, showered, dressed, and wandered downstairs through the empty house to the kitchen.

Catherine and my father looked up from the table where they were sitting, coffee cups and something that looked like waffles in front of them.

"Hi, honey," Catherine said.

"Did you get enough sleep?" my father said.

"Sure, I got enough sleep," I said.

"You must have been pretty tired," he said in a tone of clearly bogus concern.

"Actually I was up all night looking for UFOs," I said. "I just lay down for a minute."

"Very funny," he said.

"I'll get you some coffee," Catherine said.

"Don't bother," I said, going to the stove. At least I could pour my own cup of coffee.

"You know, some people need the most amazing amount of sleep," my father said, as if lecturing to a large audience. "Malraux once told me of a French general, it must have been Leclerc—"

"Jesus," I said, "it's only eight-thirty in the morning."

"Eight-fifty," my father said.

"I don't believe this!" I said.

"There's nothing wrong with being tired," my father said.

"I am not *tired*."

"Good," my father said.

I could see Catherine looking at me with what I think is called a reserved expression. "Your father asked us to go for a drive," she said.

"The invitation was really to my early-rising friend here," my father said, getting up from his chair. "But I don't mind including the husband." He thrust his hands deep into his trouser pockets and peered across at me as if we were separated by a great distance, which I suppose was the case. "Shall we get the show on the road?" he said.

The three of us climbed into the cab of an old red pickup—the usual jumble of maps, matches, horse ointment, and old rags on the front seat; two hunting rifles hanging on the rack behind us—and with the old man at the wheel we bumped our way down the dirt road below the ranch, then off to the right and up a worse road, more of a Jeep trail really, that led across the rolling red hills.

"When did you get the truck?" I said, trying to make neutral conversation.

"Christ, I dunno," he said. "They come and go. This is a good one though. A Chevy."

"A Ford," said Catherine. "At least it says Ford on the dashboard."

"Then a Ford it is," he said; a man who could be accommodating when he chose to.

Perhaps it was being out in the familiar landscape that made me want to ask him about Charlie Converse. You could almost imagine him riding toward us across the red dirt. "Whatever happened to Charlie?" I said.

"Charlie who?" he said.

"Charlie Converse."

"We had some kind of trouble with him and he moved on," he said.

"What kind of trouble?" I said.

"It was a long time ago," he said, as if it was beyond memory or interest. He was driving with both hands on the wheel, which probably wasn't such a bad idea considering the condition of the trail, though it gave him a deceptive appearance of control as we racketed along. "He was like a lot of guys out here," he said. "Fact is they peak out at sixteen or seventeen. After that they lose something they never knew they had and it makes 'em funny."

"Funny?" I said.

"Sly," he said. "It makes 'em sly." He veered off to the left and we bumped and lurched across the red dirt over to where you could see the beginnings of a field—the barest beginnings of short green growth—and a couple of pickups parked this side of a wire fence. He pulled up next to them and got out.

About a hundred yards in front of us several men were standing about in the middle of the field, one of them hammering on the end of a huge length of sprinkler pipe. My father walked briskly toward them while Catherine and I followed.

"You've been very quiet," I said.

"I like it here," she said. "And I like him."

"I'm glad you do," I said.

"He's like a big old bear," she said, and took my hand, and we went over to where my father and the men were standing.

"I thought we were gonna get a new mounting,

Billy," he was saying to a skinny young man with a sunburned face and an old cowboy hat.

"J.D. says we don't need a new mounting," Billy said. "He says they can fix it with another length of pipe."

"That's right, Mr. Avery," J.D. said, older, big-bellied, with a tractor cap and sideburns.

"Bullshit you don't need a new mounting," my father said.

"You'll see, Mr. Avery," J.D. said with a sweet, not entirely confident smile. "Okay, Sánchez, turn on the water," he called to another man, shorter, dark-skinned, also in a tractor cap, who'd been standing off to one side drinking from a can of beer and looking at us.

Sánchez stepped over to a thick white canvas hose running across the ground, squatted down, still holding his beer, and turned a spigot so that water started slowly hissing, then sputtering, then sprinkling out of holes in the long pipe, which in turn began gradually to revolve above the field.

"Looking good," said Billy Gaines.

"I think we got it fixed," J.D. said.

But no sooner did he say so than one end of the rotating pipe began to wobble on its axis, then dip, then finally bang down into the earth, continuing to spout water.

"It's been a problem with the terrain," J.D. said.

"Turn off the fucking water," my father snapped. "Do you think we're giving the stuff away?" He turned to the big man, J.D. "It's not a problem with the terrain," he said. "It's a problem because you put it in wrong."

"Mr. Avery, we put it in according to the specifications," J.D. said. "Billy watched us."

"I hire Billy to fix fence, not to install sprinklers," my father said.

"We done it according to the measurements," J.D. said.

"Don't give me that shit about measurements," my father said. "If you did it according to the measurements, the measurements were wrong. I'm sure as hell not paying for a sprinkler system that runs itself into the ground."

"You signed a contract," J.D. said.

"Sure, I signed a contract," he said, "and when you fulfill it I'll pay. All you have to do is remount the damn thing and do it right."

As he started to walk back to the fence, the man who'd been working the water spigot signaled to him and said something out of earshot. My father stopped. "What is it, Sánchez?" he said impatiently, not moving. Sánchez came toward him, no longer holding his beer can, hands in pockets; an older man than the others, middle-aged, stocky, with a little round belly. I couldn't hear what they were talking about, but then my father said something like, "I don't give a rat's ass about your problems," and continued on his way, while Sánchez stood there, watching him go, then slowly turned on his heels, his back to all of us, hands still in pockets.

We were all pretty quiet in the truck. My father

started the engine and headed us back the way we'd come. I wondered what Catherine was thinking. I could still see J.D.'s broad sideburned face trying to manage an ingratiating smile—a big man trying not to look like a fool. "I should never have given that job to J. D. Skinner," my father said. "Probably never be much of a field anyway."

"He must be new around here," I said.

"Everybody's new around here," he said. "God knows where they come from. People just drifting about like tumbleweed."

"It looked like he was trying," Catherine said.

"Trying isn't goddamn *enough*!" he said with sudden passion, both hands gripping the steering wheel.

We drove on a while more in silence until Catherine sat up and pointed out the window on my father's side. "Look!" she said excitedly. "Look over there!"

About two hundred yards away, on a rise in the ground, stood a dun-colored animal, motionless, looking at us. Then it moved a few steps. "A coyote," I said.

My father stopped the truck. "I've never seen a coyote," Catherine said. "Are there lots of them around here?"

"They're plentiful enough," my father said. He turned in his seat and took down one of the rifles from the rack behind us. Catherine and I both watched as he opened the compartment in front of him, took out two cartridges, and loaded the rifle.

"What are you going to do?" Catherine said.

"Lean back a little," he said to her over his shoulder.

He put the rifle out the open window, sighted down the barrel—the coyote was already moving off slowly to the right—and fired. *Crack!* Catherine jumped in her seat. "Oh, my God," she said. The coyote dropped in mid-stride, not so much as a quiver. My father pumped out the empty cartridge, letting it fall out the window, and returned the rifle to its place in the rack. Then he started up the truck and we drove on again in silence, a different kind of silence.

"You think I shouldn't have shot him?" he said finally to Catherine.

"I don't know," Catherine said in a small voice, staring straight ahead.

He laughed, a loud bark of a laugh. "By damn, you think I shouldn't have shot that coyote!" he said. "What does my son the philosopher think?"

"I think it was your land and your gun," I said, "but not your coyote."

"I guess it is now," he said.

As we drove I stroked Catherine's arm to be tender to her, but all she said was, "You don't have to do that," her voice clear as a bell again, almost impatient, though it seemed to me her arm was shivering.

A thin dry wind blew in the afternoon, almost no wind at all, although the ranch house creaked like a ship under sail. If you kept the bedroom door open you could hear my father downstairs talking on the telephone or else bullying Trent. "Do I have to do everything around here myself?" I heard him say at one point. But then I closed the door. For a time I tried to work on my notes, seated at the table near the window, while Catherine sitting up on the bed wrote in her journal. Then we were both lying on the bed, side by side, still wearing our clothes, eyes closed, like campers resting after a steep climb. Far away you could hear the faint drone of a little plane passing above the valley. I've never in my life—not in the army, not at school, not when Tessa left—known a place as lonely as that ranch could be in summer. Nothing ever *happens* here, I used to think. Nothing could or will ever happen here. Most every afternoon my mother would go for a walk—"her" walk. I'm going for my walk, she'd say as if it were an article of possession. Standing there in front of the house wearing a gingham blouse and khaki walking shorts and dusty brown hiking boots and some kind of floppy hat on her head which always made her look a bit comical. A couple of times each summer I went with her but mostly she went alone. I need my exercise, she'd say as if she needed to explain to someone. We all need our exercise, she'd say, tramping over the dry hills on sun-browned slender legs that never seemed to get any stronger no matter how many walks she took.

I don't know how long I slept. I didn't really mean to sleep or need to sleep, but when I awoke Catherine was gone from the room. I threw some water on my face and went downstairs. The door to my father's study was closed. Trent was nowhere to be seen. Out of old habit I went into the kitchen, where Maria was seated at the white metal table, a bunch of carrots in front of her, trailing long green stems. "Hi, Maria," I said. She looked up and nodded as if she hadn't quite heard me. "Have you seen Catherine?" I said. "She not here," Maria said—an exasperating blend of curtness and placidity. "Thanks, Maria," I said. "She go out the door," Maria said, starting to cut the stems off the carrots.

I couldn't see anyone on the road or near the house, so I took what I thought was the obvious path, the one that led up the side of the hill on the left and ended at a rocky point from where you could look down the length of the valley. The trail was narrow, steep, and shambly, full of loose stones and deer droppings as it worked higher. But the climbing felt good to my city legs, and it pleased me to think that at my age I was managing it no worse than I had as a teenager. Halfway to the top I stopped to look about for Catherine. Ahead of me was the empty hillside. Below were the ranch buildings, the willow clusters near the creek, the barn with the old tin roof and corrals. A black horse was standing in the middle of the main corral—motionless as far as the eye could see a quarter mile away, save for its tail swishing flies. And to the right of the barn, sitting on the top rung of the fence, was Catherine, a red bandanna around her head. And in the doorway of the barn, half in and half out of the shade, his face hidden by a Western hat, was my father, one foot resting on a step or a stump of wood, holding something in his hand. I tried not to feel foolish being way up here while they were way down there; the truth is it made me glad to see her there, and to see them both there together. It was certainly a pretty sight, a still life in its way: the black horse now as stationary as a statue, the sturdy old barn, and Catherine perched atop the fence. I watched as my father walked out from the dark doorway of the barn and put first a bridle and then a saddle on the horse. And then Catherine got down from the fence and stood beside the horse, and with my father stooping low, and using his hands as a hoist for her foot, she clambered into the saddle—not very gracefully I admit, for I don't know that she'd ridden much before. And then holding the reins like an old riding master, he led the big black horse, with Catherine on it (legs dangling straight like a kid on a pony ride), around and around in slow, wide circles inside the corral.

But by the time I'd come back down the hill and reached the barn the scene was over. Catherine was walking away from the empty corral, up the road to the house. A few hundred yards away you could see my father on the horse making his way across an open field.

"You looked good," I said when I caught up with her.

"Oh, I didn't," she said. "I was scared to death. You have to ride with him tomorrow."

"I have to?" I said.

"I mean you should. It would be nice. I know he'd like it."

"You know it?" I said, playing with her a little, happy that she was happy.

"Of course I know it," she said. And then she stopped for a moment and we both looked back down the road—beyond the road—to where the black horse and its blue-shirted rider were climbing slowly up into the hills.

Catherine sitting on the edge of our bed, clipping her toenails. Blue running shorts, T-shirt. The taut, smooth skin on the inside of her thighs. One leg hanging down from the bed. The other leg bent at the knee, folded across her lap like a gymnast's. Long toes like a boy.

"Do you suppose he gets lonely up here?" I said.

"What do you mean?" she said. She stretched out and then reclasped her leg. "Do you mean women?"

I hadn't thought I meant women but maybe I had. "Do you really think women?" I said. I suddenly thought of Priscilla Bonaventura with her long hair and her hand pat-patting on his arm and then didn't want to think about it anymore.

"He's not that old," she said.

"He's seventy-two," I said.

She let her feet down on the floor and bent over the bed, collecting the nail clippings into a little pile on the sheet, then brushing them into her cupped hand.

We rode out together, he and I, in the early afternoon, with a warm breeze blowing down the valley and the clouds shifting overhead. I wanted Catherine to come with us but she'd have none of the idea. "You go," she said. "He wants to ride with you." We crossed the fields behind the barn and angled up into the red hills, with him out front on the black horse, forging ahead along the narrow trail, square and solid in the saddle like a Union general, tufts of white hair sticking out in back of his hat.

"You got to kick that horse along!" he growled over his shoulder.

True enough, my mount was not a speedster. Toby by name, this was an undistinguished bay gelding, sturdy and perhaps fairly strong, but on the fat side and definitely not the equal of my father's big quarter horse. I patted his thick neck to show there were no bad feelings between us, and then kicked him hard to bring us abreast of the old man.

"Looks like he's packing a little extra weight," I said.

My father seemed not to hear the remark as we moved along together side by side. But then he said, "Nobody rides 'em anymore. I mean to ride 'em. I tell Billy Gaines to ride 'em but he won't. One of these days I'm gonna ship the whole lot off to the glue factory."

"Good plan," I said.

He turned his head toward me for an instant. "I thought you were one of those liberal, do-gooder boys," he said. "Be kind to dumb animals, I-brake-for-centipedes kind of shit."

"Hell, I don't even brake for freight trains," I said.

"Very funny," he said. "Let's cut out the crap. You want to go higher up?"

"Sure," I said.

"I mean, you ready for it?" he said. "It's not Park Avenoo."

"Let's go higher up," I said.

We were already pretty far above the valley, winding up the switchback trail, climbing past the red foothills, red rocks, red crumbly dirt, into the rolling sage-green hills that rose behind the ranch. Here was cooler air and short dry grass; scrub oak and stands of skinny pine and groves of aspen in the hollows.

"You got to kick him along!" my father called.

"Right," I said.

We were midway through a little wood—an airy, messy place full of pine needles, downed timber, and squirrels foraging in the underbrush—when the hail started to fall. First the sound, the rat-tat-tat as of pellets being flung against the leaves and tree trunks, and then the sight of round white hailstones landing on the ground, and sometimes with a sharp sting on shoulders or back. For some reason I remembered a story of Charlie Converse's, about him or someone being caught up in the mountains when a hailstorm hit and getting knocked right off his horse—"knocked plumb unconscious" was how he put it, being partial to picturesque cowboy speech whenever he had a sympathetic audience.

The old man was halted under the branches of a scrub oak and I came up beside him. "What really happened with Charlie Converse?" I said.

"What do you mean what really happened?"

"You said he got into some kind of trouble."

"You mean what kind of trouble?" he said. "He was a con artist, a chiseler, a penny-ante chiseler. All the time your mother thought he was so damn great. Saddle blankets and bridles. Stuff from the toolshed. I think he even had some deal going with that no-chin Bernard at the Texaco station."

"Saddle blankets and bridles?" I said. "Stuff from the toolshed?"

"Damn right," he said. "Nickel-and-dime stuff, except for my Mexican saddle. He was a nickel-and-dimer. You ever hear the expression?"

"I don't believe it," I said.

"You better believe it," he said, and moved out from under the shelter of the trees. "Come on, let's get the show on the road."

Fortunately the hail had pretty much stopped as we came out of the wood onto a great green plateau that stretched for several miles toward a distant tree line. The high meadow we used to call it: a broad undulating expanse of short stubby grass, with the clouds passing right overhead, and the hazy mass of the blue mountains spread out to the north. It always felt like being at the top of the world.

I could sense him looking at me, studying me in some way.

"We'll have a run," he said quietly, horse and rider motionless on the edge of the meadow.

"Well, okay," I said, mindful that this was my first time on a horse in years.

"You got a problem?" he said.

"No, no problem," I said.

He kicked his horse forward, and I took off with him, or just behind him, both animals flying across the meadow at a canter, a smooth, surging Western lope—even old Toby pounding along in the rear like an overweight Indian pony.

I watched him up ahead. Not elegant, God knows, in baggy trousers and flapping windbreaker; not one of your Argentinian equestrian-team colonels. But in a way he had his own style: strong and indelicate as a quarter horse himself. No doubt who was in control. No doubt of his getting the job done. No doubts at all.

We were traveling fast, coming up a rise in the meadow. A cold wind blowing, stinging the face. Dark clouds racing above us. Unmelted hailstones littering the ground like mothballs. I slowed down a little going up, thinking he might have halted on the other side, but no, there he was, thirty or forty yards in front, shoulders hunched forward, elbows pumping, riding hell-for-leather down the slope.

We went down and up and down again. The ground grew rough. Little obstacles everywhere; little dangers. Ruts in the field. Animal holes.

He stopped for a moment atop another hillock. I could feel him breathing hard, could see the red in his eyes from the wind, though there was no sweat on his face.

"You can't let him boss you around," he said.

"He's a little out of shape," I said, "and so am I."

"Well, this is the way to get in shape," he said, tugging his hat forward on his head. "You're not tired or something?"

"Not that tired," I said.

"Then let's get cracking," he said.

We took off again, running more or less side by side across the flat, past scattered rocks and stones, past a fallen tree trunk, past a huge granite boulder that I remember my mother once telling me had been put there by God. My father's horse was now going at full gallop over the short grass, and without my kicking him Toby picked up the pace too, snorting and panting like a crazy thing. You could feel a certain craziness in the air just then, in the wind and weather and the wildness of the place—in that sense of something coming close to the limits of control.

He was bent low over his horse and his legs were

moving. Christ, he's spurring him, I thought. He's kicking him faster. He thinks we're in a goddamn race.

About a half mile ahead were the trees, like a barrier, or like a finish line. Come on, Toby, I said, or some such thing, though speaking mostly to myself. But as we sped along I remembered also from years ago that there was something else out there between us and the tree line, something to watch out for if you were of a mind to run the meadow. Indeed there they were: the ditches. A couple of old irrigation ditches, long unused or never used (the remains of a Spanish rancher's dream of bringing water from a mountain spring): substantial ridges of grassy earth crossing the meadow a hundred yards in front of us. I was sure he'd stop or at least slow down before we reached them. But then, looking at him flying on ahead, I was just as sure he wouldn't, and that I'd be following him.

He headed straight for the first ditch and jumped it easily as far as I could tell, with me not far behind, though not clearing it quite as well—landing clumsily on the other side. In my head I could hear Charlie Converse's voice, back on those hot, boring afternoons when he was trying to teach me how to ride: "Come on, boy, keep your eyes out front of you, and don't *ever* let me see you grab that saddle horn like a dude!" I watched the old man take the second ditch. Up and over. Swaying a little in the saddle as he landed, but pretty good. As Toby and I charged forward, I willed myself to make it over, to do as well, to do better—at least to hang on with my knees and not to clutch, and I guess I managed that, or we did, for by then I was in fact so tired that Toby was doing most of the work. And then I saw the third ditch, for of course there'd been a third ditch all along, set back from the first two, nearer the trees, with the ridge of dirt a trifle higher and the trough a trifle wider.

The old man sailed over it. The big black horse high in the air. Stones and dirt churned up behind its hooves. I felt Toby pounding beneath me; felt helpless, angry, weak in the legs, afraid. Afraid of the jump, afraid not to jump. We went up all wrong. I knew it from the start. Toby off-stride. Myself too cautious, first pulling back, then far too forward, knees not holding, clutching the saddle horn like the kid I never wanted to be again. And then I fell.

There's that awful moment on the ground, when the wind is knocked out of you, and you think you'll have to lie there forever, dazed and doubled up and gasping for air. But then the moment passes: the lungs painfully fill out again; the world painfully swims back in focus.

My shoulder ached, my ass was sore.

Toby was standing a few feet away, chewing the short grass.

My father was down near the trees, astride his black horse.

"Your saddle slip?" he said when I'd remounted and caught up with him.

"No, I slipped," I said.

"I guess you did," he said.

We took a game trail down through the trees, back down the red hills, back across the fields and into the corral by the time the weather had moved off to the east and the sky was clear once more. We unsaddled and let the horses out without either of us saying much of anything, and then he went into the barn to fuss around in the tack room, and I walked back to the house and up the stairs to our room. I lay on the bed without even taking off my boots.

"I saw you coming back," said Catherine, entering the room with a bunch of wildflowers in her hand. "Did you go far?"

"Pretty far."

"You looked great together on your horses."

I sat upright on the bed. "He's a bastard," I said.

"What are you talking about?" she said as if I'd slapped her.

"I mean he's a crazy bastard," I said. "He was trying to kill me."

Catherine was clutching the wildflowers in front of her. "That's not true!" she said. "I know that's not true!"

"It's always been true," I said, falling back on the bed. I don't know which made me angrier, that I'd wiped out at the ditch or that Catherine was about to cry. It didn't seem fair somehow that she was the one about to cry, although I didn't know how to tell her that either.

I've rarely seen the old man as cheerful and affable —nay, as charming—as he was at dinner that evening. Another of his quicksilver transformations you might say. Gone were the old black pants (which I was beginning to think he slept in), the work shirt and boots, and in their place were some splendid rumpled white linen trousers, sandals, plus a long, whitish, tunicky sort of thing, the effect part priestly cassock, part Mexican beachboy. Gone too was the surly Civil War general of our disastrous afternoon, with his growl and scowl and stern manner, now supplanted by the beaming, hospitable, silver-haired grandee at the head of our table. Granted we had a guest for dinner and perhaps that was the cause of all the graciousness, but I doubt it. "Miss Sharon Posner from the university" was how my father introduced her to us: a small, big-chested young woman in bright-pink T-shirt and bluejeans, with a pale mousy face, a mountain of frizzy hair, and a tape recorder, for she had apparently driven over from the county college to interview the great man (who I suspect had forgotten the appointment) and then had been asked to stay for eats.

The meal itself was even odder than usual. No cold ham and beans that night; instead a large ornate platter of something fried, very seriously fried, in batter and bread crumbs and whatnot, that might well have been pork chops or might not have been. Also tortillas and hot peppers which were pretty good. Also an aluminum baking dish of undercooked potatoes. Also the classic Maria salad, generous in terms of iceberg lettuce, large chunks of carrot, and sweet, sticky, orange-colored dressing, and for some reason served that evening in a quite beautiful, cracked, old Lowestoft bowl. My father not only ate everything that came his way with impressive gusto, despite the banging of plates and serving dishes around him and the up-and-down nature of the repast, but between mouthfuls (and sometimes in spite of them) managed to charm or confuse or outtalk everyone in the room. Not that the rest of us gave him much competition, for Trent was austere as always, and I wasn't much better (my shoulder and pride both smarting), and even Catherine, after a few early attempts at bright, unnatural chatter, seemed cool and withdrawn. That left it to little Miss Posner, with her film-school solemnity, to serve as straight man.

"Mr. Avery," I seem to remember her saying, putting the tape recorder on the table, "would you care to comment on the film actor today?"

My father gave a learned, thoughtful flourish to his

eyebrows. "Well, you've got some good people," he said. "No doubt about it. Some very good people. That Newman guy is all right."

"Paul Newman," Miss Posner said aloud.

"That Redford guy is good," my father said, "only he never works. Hell, you read all this stuff about how awful the old studio system was, but I'm telling you a guy like Redford would have made thirty or forty pictures by now for Zanuck or Warner. What was that picture he made about the horse—you know, riding around with a bunch of electric lights on his fanny?"

"*The Electric Horseman*," said Trent, offering the information while disassociating himself from the conversation.

"Exactly right!" my father said. "Well, you sure don't have to sit on a rock in Utah or wherever to dream up *The Electric Horseman*."

"What do you think of Dustin Hoffman's work, Mr. Avery?" Miss Posner said.

"He's okay," my father said. "He's okay when he's not being nervous. Sometimes I get him confused with that other guy."

"What other guy is that, Mr. Avery?" Miss Posner said, looking up.

"He means Al Pacino," said Trent.

"Exactly right!" my father said. "Pacino. I'm telling you both those guys are too damn nervous. I've seen that Pacino do a scene like he's got ants crawling around in his underwear. Twitchy-twitchy!" Here my father wriggles around on his chair imitating a man with ants crawling around in his underwear. "Know what I mean?"

"I see," Miss Posner said. "How do you rate Robert De Niro, Mr. Avery?"

"Oh, very talented," my father said. "Definitely very talented."

"Many people consider him the most intelligent of the current actors," Miss Posner said.

"Bullcrap," my father said.

Miss Posner looked a bit startled. "You don't agree, Mr. Avery?"

My father leaned toward her, now placing a patriarchal hand on her arm and grinning like a tiger. "Dear Miss Posner," he began softly, "there are good actors and bad actors. There are poor actors and rich actors. There are thin actors and fat actors, and drunk actors and even sober actors. But show me a really *intelligent* actor and I'll show you a horse that can do algebra!" He suddenly shouted back over his shoulder. "Hey, Maria!"

Maria appeared in the doorway, solid and unruffled.

"Let's have some more of these tortillas," he said.

"No more tortillas," Maria said.

"Goddamit, I know there's more back there," he said.

"No more," she said.

He returned to Miss Posner. "Look, that Marlon Brando was supposed to be smart, but what did he do? He turned himself into a balloon. Rex Harrison was supposed to be smart, and I'll say this for him, he didn't turn himself into a balloon or talk a lot of malarkey about Zen Buddhism. But I don't see Rex ever being serious competition for Einstein." He picked up the bottle of wine and poured some more for Miss Posner, then for Catherine, then into his own glass. "If you ask me," he said, "there was only one great actor who had any real brains."

"Sir Laurence Olivier?" said Miss Posner warily.

"No, I don't mean *Sir* Laurence Olivier," he said.

"Orson Welles?" she said.

"I certainly don't mean Orson Welles," he said. "There's another balloon for you. I was talking about Buster Keaton."

"Did you say Buster Keaton?" Miss Posner said.

"They used to call Chaplin the King," he said. "Then Gable was the King. I don't know who they say is the King now. Maybe they don't have Kings anymore."

"Meryl Streep," said Trent.

"Kings or Queens," my father said. "They come and go. But let me tell you, Keaton was the King of them all. He was the best. Jesus, how he could move —like a track star, like a fucking ballet dancer. And that face: better than Helen of Troy. And smart too —the brains of an inventor. There wasn't anything he couldn't do. Make you laugh or make you cry . . ."

Just then Maria stalked in from the kitchen, bearing a chocolate cake that looked as if it had been dropped from a great height. She put it down in front of my father, who helped himself to an enormous piece and shoved what was left of it down the table.

"You know, I met him once," he said.

"Let me change cassettes," Miss Posner said.

"This was when I was a young guy starting out in Hollywood," he said, speaking largely to Catherine. "A bunch of us drove over to Venice one Saturday afternoon. It must have been a Saturday because everyone was out walking on the boardwalk, and there was a band in one of the casinos—open-air casinos is what they were—and people were dancing. I remember someone in our group dug me in the ribs and said, 'Hey, isn't that Buster Keaton over there?' I looked over where he was pointing, and there sitting at a little table not far from the dancing was Buster Keaton all by himself. I mean back when I didn't know anything about movies I knew about Buster Keaton. I think the first movie I ever saw was a Buster Keaton feature. My ma took me to Chicago on the train and we saw *Sherlock Junior*. Well, there he was, just setting there all alone, nobody recognizing him, watching the people dance and drinking from a little bottle with a straw in it. So I got up my nerve and walked over to him. 'Hi there, Mr. Keaton,' I said, 'I'm a real fan of yours.' I was gonna say from Illinois but that sounded bush. 'Well, is that so?' he said. His face was deadpan like in the movies, so you couldn't tell what was going through his mind. 'What are you drinking?' I said. 'I'm drinking lemonade,' he said. 'I always like a good lemonade on a warm afternoon.' I could see the bottle was near empty so I said, 'Well, can I buy you another lemonade?' He didn't change his expression any, but he motioned me over to the empty chair at the table. 'Might as well have a seat if you're buying,' he said. So I sat down and called over the waitress and ordered two lemonades, even though I'd just been drinking beer, and then we just sat there drinking our lemonades and listening to the music and watching the people dance. It was like we'd known each other all our lives. When he finished his lemonade he pushed his chair back and stood up. 'It's been a real pleasure,' he said, 'but I have appointments.' He said it just like that: 'I have appointments.' And then he was gone. Let me tell you, I've sometimes thought of all the questions I wanted to ask him but didn't."

"Why didn't you?" said Catherine, very soft.

"I guess he didn't seem the kind of man you asked a lot of questions of," my father said.

I was aware of Catherine across the table, silent, amazingly beautiful. Her eyes downcast. Hands folded demurely on her lap. A glow, almost a radiance on her cheeks. It touched me so that she liked him; and that he liked her, was pleased by her. After dinner we all sat together for a while in the living room, having coffee. Then Miss Posner left, and Maria too, driven down the road I think by Trent. "Where does she go at night?" Catherine asked; she was sitting by herself at the little backgammon table (relic of an earlier period at the ranch) across the room, toying with the counters. My father stood at the wall cupboard, his back to us, looking for a cigar. "I think she lives in town," I said. He turned around, puffing his cigar alight; then walked far across the room to the big window, looking out at the night, then back to where Catherine was sitting, making her little private game out of the backgammon counters.

"Do you still play?" I said to him, perhaps remembering the occasional evenings he and my mother used to play together at that table.

"Backgammon?" he said, as if barely hearing me. "Hell, no."

"It seems to me you were pretty good," I said. I could feel her eyes on me from a distance. "You and Catherine ought to have a game together."

"Oh, not me," Catherine said.

"Come on," I said.

"No, please," she said, smiling, shy.

"You told me once you liked to play," I said.

"Why are you *doing* this?" she said.

My father's thoughts returned from wherever they'd been roaming. He looked down at her, then pulled out the other chair and sat opposite her across the table. "Okay, kid, let's see who's the champ," he said, beginning to set out his counters on the board.

"Okay, you're on," she said, coolly arranging hers.

The room was dark and peaceful as they played; I don't know how many games, three or four maybe, my father winning most of them. But the only noise came from the clink of counters and the tumbling dice, for they were both serious players who rarely talked; and I for my part was content not to disturb them—was content to breathe the still air, and even the cigar smoke, and watch the old man happy for a change.

In the dream I had that night I'm walking down a gray hallway inside an ancient building (a medieval castle it seems like), past gray stone walls, tapestries, flickering torches, then up stone steps, a winding staircase, moving slowly, almost in slow motion, moving warily like a detective, down a long white corridor, brightly lit, bare and blank, without ornament, without windows, smooth and featureless as a movie set. The corridor goes on forever, silent, turning this way, that way. There's a door placed in a wall. A room beyond it. A series of rooms, connected, one behind the other. Inside, the light is somber, faint, like winter's light, like twilight. Thick curtains. Wood paneling. The furniture is old-fashioned—perhaps Victorian. There's a smell of age and old things in these rooms as I pass through them, pass through an open doorway into the last room. Here is thick darkness, also dread. Dimly my eyes make out a long low couch, a chaise longue with a woman's dress lying half on, half off it; a woman's slip discarded on the floor; a straight-back chair on which a man's jacket has been neatly hung—a military jacket of some description, with braid and epaulets. Now the darkness fills the room like fog, billowing around me, making me fearful, making me afraid to look, to turn my head. But I turn it anyway, toward the bed, the double bed I know is there—shadowy, with rumpled sheets, with two people lying on the sheets. It's hard to see the man: naked, face down, bare legs and buttocks and back. It's harder still to see the woman beside him—naked also, one arm thrown back against the pillow, pale creamy thighs, soft breasts, long hair covering her face. I take a step forward, but then the darkness covers everything, the bed, the man and woman on the bed, the room, covers me too and I wake up, gasping for air, my heart pounding, shaken—though not so much from fear, it feels like, as from having come so close to finding what I'd been looking for.

Catherine brought me coffee in the morning while I was working. Or trying to work. Or pretending to work.

"Can we go see the rock paintings today?" she said.

"Who told you about the rock paintings?"

"He did," she said. "Sam."

It was strange to hear her call him Sam. His name, of course. All the world called him Sam.

"You go," I said.

"What do you mean?" she said.

"You two go."

"*We* two?" She was standing in the middle of our room. "I wanted to go with *you*."

"I have to work," I said.

She started to tie on her red headband. Arms raised. Elbows forming triangles.

"We could go this afternoon," she said. "When you've finished."

The skin white under her arms.

I knew she was only trying to be sweet.

"Thanks for the invitation," I said.

"Tom, it's not an *invitation*!"

She went to the dresser, picked up something, put it down, picked up something else, the car keys I think, put them in her pocket, turned around.

"Did you have a fight with him the other day?" she said.

"No," I said.

Her face was so serene and unclouded in the morning light.

"Couldn't you just talk to him instead of getting mad?" she said. "Couldn't you just talk to him?"

I didn't know what to say. *I've never been able to talk to him in my life.*

"Well, okay," she said. "I'll get out of your hair." I watched her walk across the floor and out the door, thinking please don't go, don't go.

Sometime around noon, with the house empty and quiet, I found my father outside dragging a length of fence pole down the hill toward the pump house.

"You want a hand?" I said.

"What for?" he said.

He dropped the pole with a thud next to a pile of logs, tree branches, and so forth, kicking it forward with his feet. "Billy Gaines was supposed to saw this stuff into firewood but he never does shit around here anymore," he said.

"You ever eat lunch?" I said.

"*Lunch?*" He looked at me as if he were hearing the word for the first time in his life.

"I thought maybe we could sit down together and talk," I said. "I guess the meal itself isn't all that important."

But he'd already started back to the house at a fairly brisk clip. I followed him inside to the kitchen, where he went to the fridge, peered in, took out something wrapped in old tinfoil, sniffed it, and put it back. Then a plastic container filled with something yellow, which he opened, stuck his finger in, and tasted. "Could be egg salad," he said, putting it on the counter behind him. Then he took out two cans of cold beer, handed me one, opened his, took a swig from it, and headed off again, this time through the dining room and the main room and out a small door to what we used to call the back porch even though it was in the front of the house.

"How's this?" he said, sitting down in an old rocking chair.

"Fine," I said.

He put his beer down on a weather-worn little table and picked up a flyswatter, which he started to tap impatiently against his leg. "Maybe you'd like it better inside," he said.

"No, it's fine out here," I said, sitting down in an equally old wicker chair nearby.

He leaned back in the rocker as if trying out the idea of taking his ease, then abruptly sat forward, frowning out across the grassy area in front of us. "That damn wall's falling all to pieces!" he said indignantly, standing up, dropping the flyswatter on the floor beneath him, and then he strode down the steps of the porch and off across the scrubby grass with me more or less dutifully at his heels.

Of course, the wall! I had forgotten about the wall. It was about three feet high—in some places more, in some places less—and was built out of what I guess you'd call local rock, hand-laid by my father and someone else (Charlie Converse, in fact!), both of them hefting and cursing together through the afternoons of a long-ago summer. My father was now down on his hands and knees beside it, wedging pieces of the crumbly stone back into the gaps from which they'd fallen.

"It's really stood up pretty well," I said, hoping to strike a positive note, getting down on my hands and knees beside him and searching the thistle grass for errant rocks.

"Wasn't ever laid right," he said. He glanced over in my direction. "What in hell are you doing?"

"I'm putting these back in the wall," I said.

"They don't belong *there*," he said. "They'll only fall out again if you put 'em in *there*. You've got to put 'em in where they belong. Like this . . ." He forcibly removed one of the rocks from where I'd placed it and shoved it in farther up, where he'd been working.

"I remember when you built the wall," I said.

"Goddamn crazy idea of your mother's," he said. "Look at these thistles everywhere! No wonder the wall doesn't hold up." He pulled the front of his shirt out of his pants, wrapped it around his hand, and yanked a thistle out of the ground.

"I didn't know it was her idea," I said.

"Who in hell else would want a wall in a place like this?" he said. "*Wouldn't a stone wall just be lovely over there!*" he said in a not very faithful imitation of my mother's voice. He pulled himself to his feet, the front of his shirt hanging down like an apron.

"It looks good," I said.

"It looks like hell," he said, and started off in the direction of the toolshed.

Inside the toolshed, which was just as I remembered

it—the little-used or never-used implements hanging overhead in meticulous array and everything else in complete disorder—he rummaged around, first here, then there, tossing rusty sprinkler heads on the floor, pushing pieces of an old lawn mower out of the way with his boots.

"You can never find a goddamn thing here when you want it," he said.

"What are you looking for?" I said.

"I'm looking for some goddamn hedge clippers to clip those thistles," he said. "What did you think I was looking for?"

"How about these?" I said.

He turned and examined what I held out to him as if it were some kind of dead animal. "That's a *gardening* thing," he said scornfully, "for *flowers*." He looked back in the drawer he was currently ransacking, pulled out some pieces of pipe, several large fence nails, flung them into a nearby barrel, then said, "Okay, we'll try it."

Back outside, both of us on our knees beside the wall, my father clips the marauding thistles with the garden clippers, which seem more than adequate for the job (doubtless having been purchased for that purpose), but not content with leaving the thistles where they fall he must fling them behind him in the direction of the road.

"I could get a wheelbarrow," I said.

"What for?" he said.

"To get the thistles out of the way," I said.

"The thistles?" he said. "Who gives a flying fuck

about the thistles? They're not going anywhere. I thought you wanted to talk."

I thought yes, I wanted to talk, but you could no more sit still and listen to someone than you could fly to the moon.

"Well, I thought it was a good idea at the time," I said. "But you seem to have a lot of things to do."

"Putting rocks back in the wall?" he said. "Pulling up a couple of thistles? You call that having things to do? You think that's how I spend my time?"

"Not really," I said. "Just the last half hour."

"Buddy, I was only waiting for you," he said. "Believe you me, I've got better things to do than pull up thistles in my front yard."

"Look, I know that," I said. "But we can talk some other time."

"Why not now?" he said. "You got any gloves with you?"

"No," I said.

"Damn," he said. Then, "That rosebush better come out." He was glowering in the direction of a cluster of wild rosebushes—each one bearing a fearsome armament of thorns—while at the same time winding his shirttail around the palm of his hand.

"I don't think you want to try that," I said.

"There's a way of doing it," he said.

He reached out and grabbed one of the branches with his shirt-covered hand, then pulled and pulled, and—presto—the thing came out of the ground. I looked to see how his hand had survived: without a scratch, so it would seem.

"That's very impressive," I said.

"Impressive my ass," he said. He got slowly to his feet and appeared to be scanning the horizon, doubtless for other sections of the landscape to tear down or reassemble or move or kick or toss over his shoulder. "When are you going to write the big book?"

"I don't know," I said. "I never thought writing for size was the point."

"Oh, don't give me that smarty-pants bullshit," he said.

"I mean it," I said. "I don't see that big, thick books are any better than—"

"You know what I'm talking about," he said. For some reason one of his eyebrows was curling wildly upward in what might have been a comical effect. "When are you going to write a book for people to read?"

"Oh, Jesus," I said. I didn't know whether to laugh or cry.

"You don't need Jesus," he said. "You got too much Jesus in you as it is."

"Thanks," I said.

"You've got to reach people," he said. "Where they eat and fart and fuck and everywhere else. How many copies of that tree book did you sell anyway?"

"If you mean *Northwest Territories*," I said, "it had two printings and won the Jennings Medal."

"I wasn't asking about printings and medals," he said.

"Twenty-five thousand hardcover," I said. "I don't know how much in paperback."

"How about that gloom-and-doom utility book?" he said.

"If you mean *Shad River No. 3*," I said, "I'm really proud of that book."

"How many copies?" he said.

"For Christ sakes, thirty thousand." Actually, it had been closer to 23,400 when I last checked, but my publisher had been well pleased with it and so was I.

"Thirty thousand?" he said. "You couldn't fill half of Yankee Stadium with thirty thousand." He bent over and picked up the clippers. "These aren't worth shit," he said.

"Are you finished?" I said.

"Finished?" he said. "Damn right I'm finished. I got work to do. You coming?"

"Not right now," I said.

"Suit yourself," he said, and off he went across the grass to the house, leaving me at the wall—his and Charlie Converse's and I guess my mother's wall, though undeniably his wall in the end.

Catherine coming up the road past the barn. Blue-jeans water-soaked below the knees as if she'd been wading. Sneakers in one hand. A fishing rod in the other.

"Look what I found in the downstairs closet," she said. Happy as a kid.

It was an old bamboo fly rod that I think had once belonged to my mother's sister, Aunt Helena, or one of her men friends.

"Do you think it's okay to use it?" she said.

"I expect it is."

"Oh, good," she said. Her feet were covered with mud and flecks of grass. "My feet are filthy," she said.

"We had a talk," I said. "He thinks I don't write big enough books."

"Big enough?" she said. "What do you mean?"

"Best sellers," I said. "I don't write enough best sellers. I don't write any best sellers. I can't fill Yankee Stadium."

"Yankee Stadium?" she said. "I don't understand."

"Look, you got me into this," I said. "*Talk* to him, you said. *Talk* to him. If Attila the Hun showed up, you'd want me to go and *talk* to him."

"Your father isn't Attila the Hun."

"They seem to ride about the same."

"I don't know what's gotten into you," she said. "You're a good writer. You've written some very good books."

"Thanks, but I've just about had it," I said.

"You've had it?"

"I mean I've had it with him. I'm about ready to leave."

"Now you're really getting crazy, Tom," she said, walking beside me, clutching the fishing rod in her tight hand.

But of course I wasn't crazy and we didn't leave, at least not then. After all, how can a grown man, a certifiable adult (nearly forty years old!) suddenly walk out, just like that, and with his young wife in tow, for no better reason than that he can't get on with his aged father? No, I hadn't come all that way, traveled all those miles and years, to blow everything now by acting like a child. "Don't act like such a *child*!" I remember my mother saying to me when she was especially disappointed or vexed by something I'd done; the cold, deep, angry way she said the word *child* then was always a surprise. Even so, the awful truth was that with every passing hour at the ranch I felt, if not more childish, more kid-like, then secretly tugged backward in time like a swimmer caught in an undertow, being pulled slowly out to sea: the safe shoreline of maturity and marriage receding before my eyes, while behind me stirred the dark and murky waters of nameless old dangers.

. . .

I say secretly because I tried hard to hide the change—my drifting out to sea—from Catherine and my father. It was a strangely passive time (not unlike childhood in its way), though for the most part I think we all coexisted in a harmony of sorts, a deceptive equilibrium, the three of us moving about the ranch like planets in our different courses, sometimes close but rarely touching.

I worked and didn't work. I abandoned the Filipachi book as unimportant. Then took it up again. I scribbled six pages of a screenplay version, each page sillier than the last, then threw the lot away. I couldn't decide the simplest things.

Meanwhile, downstairs, the serious business of the house proceeded apace. Major-league stuff, as some would say. I was under the impression that my father stayed in his office much of the day, and was also in there late at night. Sometimes you could hear his harsh muffled voice on the phone, speaking to important people in New York or Los Angeles or conducting long script conferences with Donald Newcome, his big Hollywood screenwriter. Sometimes there was only the clackety-clack of his old Underwood. Other times there was no sound at all, which wasn't the same as silence. I felt him in there behind the closed door, a general with his maps and scouting reports, preparing for the next great campaign.

Trent left silently one morning. Houston. On business. My father didn't say what business and I didn't ask.

. . .

As for Catherine, my precious Catherine, I think she was never more beautiful than in those hot, dry, sun-baked, stretched-out days. In fact her city glow—that glossy, pretty, stunning look—had nearly faded from her face, as if scoured from her cheeks and eyes by sun and dust, and in its place was something flatter, plainer, less pretty you might say, but more compelling. Now that she had her fishing rod she spent hours walking along the creek, up and down, finding places where the creek bed widened or descended in a series of pools, some as deep as your waist, some as shallow as saucers. I asked her if she wasn't lonely, doing that. But she said, "No, I'm not lonely." One of the first afternoons I sat on the bank and watched her cast. She did it well too; at least it looked as if she knew what she was doing: the slender bamboo rod bending against the sky, the line whipping back and forth through the air.

"You're very good," I said, my heart melting. "When did you learn to do that?"

"Poppa taught me," she said. Serious as a country girl.

We drove out to see the rock paintings. On the side of a cliff across the valley. In the shadow of the mountains. The rock walls pink and orange, reaching straight up two hundred feet or so. Even in the glare of sunlight the paintings had a ghostly look about them. Childish figures for the most part, half rubbed off by time and weather, though clearly not made by children. Two wolf-like animals floating upside down. A caped woman with circles for breasts. A large figure with a mask for a face, holding a wand or spear. "What do you think?" I said to Catherine, who was walking around in silence at the foot of the cliff.

"I don't know," she said. "I don't know what they mean."

"They're like dreams," I said.

"I never had dreams like that," she said.

We stayed there longer than either of us wanted to, walking around in the harsh sunlight, squinting up at the primitive designs.

A snake like a coil of rope.

Three figures in a row. Stick figures. Round moon faces. Arms waving in triumph or terror or abandon.

Catherine seated on a flat white boulder, looking away to the hazy mountains. Beads of sweat on her forehead, like raindrops.

"Shall we go?" I said finally.

We were walking down the path to the road. "My mother used to come here all the time one summer," I said. "She had a camera and took hundreds of photographs of the rock paintings and wanted to sell them to a magazine. But they never really looked like anything when they were developed."

"Tell me you like me," Catherine said.

"Of course I like you," I said. "I love you."

But she was silent all the way back in the car.

My father in the kitchen teaching Catherine how to make ranch coffee. "What you do is get the water boiling," he says. "We got the water boiling, right?"

"Right," says Catherine.

"Then we dump in the coffee," he says. "Like so." He shakes part of the contents of a tin of Maxwell House into the big enamel kettle. "Turn down the heat."

"What a mess!" says Catherine.

"What a mess?" he says. "This is the best damn coffee in the world. Now where's that egg?" He runs to the fridge, grabs a brown egg, brings it back and bangs it on the side of the stove and drops what remains of the insides partly in the kettle and partly on the floor. "One egg!" he says in the spirit of Escoffier detailing a fine point. "No more, no less. It doesn't have to be brown." He wipes his hand on the seat of his pants. "Now we let it sit five minutes." He marches to the sink, rinses out some dirty coffee mugs, and sets them down next to the stove. "Now we pour."

"That's not five minutes," Catherine says.

"It's close enough," he says. He tastes the coffee in the first mug, smacks his lips. "Delicious," he says, handing it to Catherine. "Isn't that the best coffee you've ever tasted?"

"Yes, it is," she says.

Catherine said, "Why did he leave your mother?"

"He didn't leave her," I said. "She left him."

"Are you sure?" she said.

"Of course I'm sure."

"I mean why did it happen?" she said. "Why did she leave him?"

"I guess there was some other girl," I said.

"Did he have a lot of girls?"

"How should I know?" I said. "Yes, I think he did."

I went riding by myself for a while each afternoon —nothing much, a little exercise for Toby and me. But one afternoon it rained, more of a thunderstorm than the usual shower, and so I drove over to the old town. Not the so-called new town where we shopped, which was no town at all but a shopping center ten miles east along the Interstate. Where I went was the old town of Santa Ana, though in this case "town" was also something of a misnomer, at least a euphemism. More a village than a town; more a ramshackle collection of adobe huts and tin-roof shacks huddled together at the far end of the valley, west not east, never much in the mainstream in the best of times but now bypassed by the new highway and, as they say on television, left to die. There was an ancient red cattle truck stopped this side of the wood bridge on the way in, tilting crazily to one side on two flat tires. An oil drum filled with trash, smoldering on a corner. The two or three narrow dirt streets were still unpaved. A main street (for some reason, now called Second Street) with a small general store, a handful of tumbledown shops, a couple of dark and dingy bars, a Texaco station apparently closed. Elsewhere trailers and little houses with wash hanging from lines, and dogs and chickens wandering about. Even though the rain had stopped the streets were empty, save for two barefoot Indian kids hitting stones with a baseball bat. Someone had dumped a pile of wooden crates in the street in front of the Farmacia-Drugs. I parked next to the general store ("Parking For Customers Only" said the old sign) and went inside. Two teenage girls, one white and pasty, the other dark-skinned, were behind the counter listening to scratchy pop music on an old radio. Years ago I remembered they used to have fishing supplies in the back and I thought of trying to get some new flies for Catherine. "Do you have any trout flies?" I asked the girls but they only giggled. I looked around vainly in what used to be the hunting section and was now clearly the giftware and hunting section: displays of dusty drinking glasses with pink Have-a-nice-day decals resting next to vicious-looking knives and shotguns. Then I bought a can of fly-wipe for Toby and started back. The two kids were now hitting an empty beer can with their bat. In front of one of the bars three Indians were sitting on a bench drinking something out of paper cups. Clearly there were some places one had no need to revisit.

I stopped at the barn on my way back to leave the fly-wipe in the tack room. As I was closing up I saw a car drive up the road and stop just beyond where I was standing. It was a car I'd seen a few times before from the house, a ten-year-old dark green Pontiac with most of its chrome missing. I'd noticed it drive up and stop at the same spot, after which Maria would get out the passenger side and walk up the rest of the way, coming in the side door off the kitchen. I'd never actually seen the driver but I always assumed it was a man. This time, once again, Maria climbed out the far side of the car and began to walk up the road, carrying in her arms a bag of groceries. Then a man got out of the driver's side and called something to her, but she either didn't hear or kept on walking. I couldn't see his face because of his straw hat and because of the distance, but he was a little man with a thick waist and silver on his belt. Maria was walking slowly up the hill and now the man began to run up the hill after her. He didn't have that far to run but he was running hard, and just as he came up behind her Maria turned around and he hit her squarely on the side of the head. You could tell it was a mean, hard blow because Maria dropped to the ground, on her knees. The man just stood in front of her. I could hear him talking to her in Spanish. Maria was half kneeling, half squatting in the middle of the wet road, the groceries lying in the dirt around her. Then he took a swipe at her with the toe of his boot. I stepped out the barn doorway and said something like "Hey there!" They both turned their heads and looked at me, and I recognized the man as the one who'd been working on the sprinkler in the field—Sánchez. Now he pulled his hat low, walked down the hill, got in his car, swung it around, and drove away. By the time I reached Maria, she had picked up her groceries and was heading back up the road. "Maria!" I called. She stopped and turned around. There was a smudge of blood on the right side of her mouth; no tears. "What do you want?" she said. "Are you okay?" I said. "Yes," she said, as if to say none of your business, "okay"; and she turned her back and continued up toward the house.

Late one afternoon, just before dusk, a cloud of swallows flew in, I don't suppose from nowhere although it seemed that way. They came rushing in from the west, where the sky was still golden from the setting sun, at least fifty of them, maybe more—literally a cloud—flying tight formation twenty feet above the darkening fields; then whirled around the barn roof; then scattered like a burst of fireworks, diving, darting, swooping through the willows; then regrouped and sped off toward the eastern hills.

Catherine and I were walking in the fields beyond the barn, trying to be close, though I think each of us felt lonely with the setting sun.

"They look so happy," she said as the little birds swept by. We stopped to watch, the two of us inches from one another in the pale light, spectators at a private air show. "Poppa would have loved it here," she said.

"They say the fishing's better in Colorado," I said.

"I wasn't thinking just about the fishing," she said. "He wasn't that serious about it anyway. I mean he never really fished anywhere but at this little lake no more than twenty minutes from where we lived. You know, not real secluded. Rowboats and outboards and people swimming in the summer. But I guess he sure loved to go there."

"Did he catch any fish?" I said, not meaning it to come out quite the way it did.

"Of course he caught fish," Catherine said. "Trout. Perch. A lot of them were really big too."

"Not like here," I said.

"Nobody fishes here," she said. We were walking slowly between the willows and the road; her hands in the pockets of her jeans. "He'd always go Wednesday afternoons," she said, "after work. I don't know what was so special about Wednesdays. And sometimes he'd take me along and that's how I learned."

"He must have liked having you around," I said. I remembered a photograph of Catherine's father: a tall, thin man in a short-sleeve shirt; a handsome man with a mild, tentative expression.

"Oh, sure," she said. "I bet your dad taught you about things too."

"You wanna bet?" I said.

"Everybody's dad teaches them about things," she said.

"When I was twelve he taught me how to make a gin fizz," I said.

"What's that?" she said.

"It's a drink," I said. "When I was nine he taught

me the best way to fight Rocky Graziano. The way to do it is you keep your left high and work on the midsection."

"I don't understand," she said.

"The Zale–Graziano fight at Madison Square Garden," I said. "The third Zale–Graziano fight. The old Madison Square Garden. A very big event. Jock McClain stood him up, so he took me instead. There was a tiny old man in the seat right in front of me with a shiny bald head and rings all over his fingers, and all during the fight my dad kept leaning over to him and saying, 'The guy's gotta keep his left high,' and 'The guy's gotta work on the midsection.' Sometimes he'd remember I was there and say the same thing to me. 'The guy's gotta keep his left high . . . the guy's gotta work on the midsection.' "

"Don't, Tom," she said.

"When I was fourteen he showed me how to get the best table at '21'—"

"Don't," she said.

"You ask for Jack or maybe Mac, only it turns out you have to be my father to do it."

"Stop it, Tom!" she said, angry this time.

"What's the matter?" I said. "I thought you wanted to know what he taught me."

"I hate it when you sound like that."

"Look, it's not my fault he wasn't the kind of great old dad your Poppa was," I said.

"He's been pretty nice to us," she said. I couldn't tell whether there were tears in her eyes or not.

"He's been pretty nice to *you*."

"He's nice to you when you let him!" she said.

"Honey," I said, "even people who like my father don't think he's *nice*."

Catherine stood there shaking her head from side to side, as if to shake away what I'd said, as if to shake me away. Then she turned and began walking toward the willows and the creek. I watched her go, thinking what a strange thing to have a fight about, thinking that maybe if she communed with the stream and the fish and the spirit of her dear Poppa for a while she'd feel better about things. As I walked back up the road to the house, the fields were still, the whole earth seemed still, save for two blackbirds flapping overhead. I looked over toward the old house, settled beneath the cottonwoods, the last rays of sunlight glistening on the windows. Then I saw my father standing on the porch next to one of the wood pillars. If he saw me he gave no sign of it. He was staring back down the road, across the fields, and when I turned to follow the direction of his gaze I could see Catherine's white shirt moving through the willows to the creek.

Priscilla came by for dinner that night, but without George, who'd gone north to Colorado where he had oil rigs working. Thus we were a neat foursome around the old table. My father was never more charming, almost benign, once again mysteriously transformed from an abrupt and cantankerous old rascal into an elder statesman of sagacity and courtly good humor. At first I thought the change might be due to the presence of the elegant Mrs. Bonaventura, but he seemed scarcely to notice her, or rather he noticed her in the familiar offhand way one notices a wife of many years, or perhaps an old mistress. As for Catherine, she arrived at table quiet and withdrawn, not shy so much as remote, on her guard. She looked at me, I looked at her; but there was something brittle in her eyes, standoffish. It made me sad to think we weren't friends that evening, but I knew we would be soon again. I was frankly glad that the old man knew how to be considerate of her mood, or perhaps didn't notice it, being content instead to lecture all of us (and in generally impressive fashion) on the Cárdenas revolution he'd covered in Mexico in the thirties.

"Those goddamn oil people were everywhere," he was saying. "Standard Oil, Socony-Vacuum, all the big outfits. They wanted to take over the country. Hell, they'd already taken it over. They just never figured that Cárdenas guy meant business."

"Did you ever meet him?" Catherine said, speaking for the first time. "Cárdenas?"

"Sure I met General Cárdenas," he said. "I was going to write a book about him once."

"I didn't know you'd thought of writing a book, Sam," said Priscilla.

"A lot of people write books," he said. "Of course I'm not talking about art. I'm talking about a regular book. The facts."

"It's a wonderful idea," said Catherine.

"Some big editor in New York, Ken McCormick at Doubleday, was all set to give me a contract," he said.

"I wish you'd done it," Catherine said.

"Never had the time," he said. "I had all these notes. Interviews. Jesus, I had wonderful interviews. But I was always too damn busy, writing scripts at night and directing during the day. Anyway, there wasn't any money in books and I needed the do-re-mi."

"Tom, is that right, there's no money in books?" Priscilla said.

"I guess there's money for James Michener and Jane

Fonda and a couple of novels," I said, "but not that much for everyone else."

"I hope Tom writes a novel someday," Catherine said.

"A novel, eh?" he said. "That's major-league stuff." He was smiling at Catherine like an old cardinal. "Well, I bet you're a very effective muse."

"I wish I were," she said, looking down at her plate.

My father didn't take his eyes off her. "Don't tell me my son neglects you?" he said with mock concern.

"No," she said, "he doesn't."

"Of course they say some girls don't want to be treated all that nicely," he said.

"Really, Sam," Priscilla said.

"You don't mean that," Catherine said.

"You're right, I don't," he said. He patted Catherine's arm absently. "Tom, open us another bottle of that Beaujolais, will you?"

On my way to the sideboard I nearly collided with Maria coming in from the kitchen with a tray.

"And don't knock poor Maria down," he said.

Maria gave me her usual blank enigmatic look; sometimes I thought she simply didn't see any of us in that house. Nor was there any sign or mark upon her to show that the incident in the road had ever taken place. As I stood at the sideboard opening the wine, I caught sight of Catherine's face in the candle-light, cool and faraway.

"Catherine's a wonderful wife for a writer," I said, putting the new bottle down in front of my father.

"There's no such thing as a wonderful wife for a

writer," my father said. He seemed to be peering at all of us through spectacles.

"That's not true," Catherine said. "Besides, you don't even mean it."

"I do mean it," he said.

"You shouldn't say things you don't mean," she said. "It's wicked."

"Listen to her!" my father said with a big grin. "*It's wicked.*"

"Don't tease," Catherine said, though her eyes had suddenly come alive.

"I'm not teasing," he said. "You're absolutely right. It is wicked. Hell, I'm wicked."

"No, you're not," Catherine said.

"Don't be too sure," Priscilla said, playing grownup between the two children.

"One thing's for certain," he said. "I was never any damned good at being married."

"I bet that's not true either," Catherine said.

"Christ almighty, I had three wives and I was terrible to all three of them. I was wicked. I was worse than wicked." He beamed unrepentantly. "Isn't that right, Tom?"

"I don't know," I said.

"Tom doesn't know. Actually, Tom's mother and I had some nice times for a while," he said. "And then there was that little Esther Tobey but she was too smart to marry me."

"Only two women you were nice to?" Catherine said. "I find that hard to believe."

I thought, why do you find it so hard to believe?

But it was good to see Catherine cheerful again, no longer chilly and withdrawn. And to see him almost gentle for a change.

He pushed his chair back from the table and stood up. "Let's go next door and have some coffee," he said. "Hell, let's skip the coffee and have us some Calvados." He turned to Catherine and took her by the hand. "Princess, have you ever tasted Calvados?" he said.

"I don't think so," I heard Catherine say.

"Good," he said, "then you can learn about Calvados from me." And with one arm around Catherine and his other around Priscilla, he led the way into the other room.

After dinner everything seems suddenly quiet, suspended. Neither the Calvados nor coffee is poured. Priscilla sits on the couch, the coffee tray before her, an elegant housemother in long plaid skirt, a silky scarf around her neck. The big room is half lit: two lamps throw yellow circles on the ceiling. My father is in his study taking a phone call; the door ajar, his voice growly, indistinct. On the far side of the room, close to the wall, Catherine sits cross-legged on the floor, tinkering with an old record player. I can hear my father saying, "Herb, you think about it. I just want you to think about it, Herb." Then he puts the phone down and comes back into the room.

"Everything okay with the movie?" I say.

He's standing just this side of the doorway to his study. "Movie's going to knock their goddamn socks off," he says. Then more to Priscilla than me: "That little asshole Herbie Prochnow. Used to run Selznick's mimeograph machine." He grins and ambles over to the cupboard where he keeps his cigars.

"Sam, do you want coffee?" Priscilla asks.

He's behind her, in shadow, lighting a cigar, looking out into the room. "What are you doing there, gorgeous?" he says to Catherine, still on the floor next to the far wall.

"Trying to get this to work," she says.

"It's busted," he says. "Been busted for years. I meant to buy one of those fancy Jap machines but never got around to it."

But then somehow Catherine gets it working; at any rate, a hum comes through the speakers. She takes a record from a stack of dusty albums, also on the floor, and puts it on the turntable. Soon the scratchy sound of a 1960s-style tenor sax fills the room. Gerry Mulligan. She turns the volume down a bit, gets to her feet.

"Good girl," my father says. He's at the liquor cabinet pouring what must be Calvados into little glasses.

The room seems very peaceful then, floating somewhere in time. Catherine stays where she is, at the other end of the room, listening to the music. Her feet are bare on the dark floor. She wears a plain white blouse and a new pink skirt, a Mexican skirt it looks like, short and summery, bright pink. Her hands are clasped behind her back. Her feet move softly on the floor in time to the music. Long legs and pink skirt, swaying in and out of the shadows. It's as if she's dreaming (or maybe I'm the one who's dreaming). Everything seems very slow: the music, Catherine dancing, my father moving like a big cat across the floor toward her. He hands her a little glass of Calvados, she drinks from it and gives it back. For a moment she's standing stock-still, looking past him, looking right at me. Then I hear him say, "May I have this dance?"

She drops her eyes, turns her head. "You'll have to get rid of that cigar," she says.

He puts the cigar and glass down on the backgammon table. Then they dance. The old-fashioned way. His hand behind her back. Nothing fancy. An old man and his daughter (perhaps his granddaughter!) at a dinner dance. His white head towers above her. He seems large, almost top-heavy, though surprisingly limber from the waist down. Her legs move backward with him, turn, move forward. Her eyes stay level, straight ahead. She stumbles briefly, recovers, smiles a private smile but not at him. She doesn't look at him. The sounds of Gerry Mulligan's *Sweet Lorraine* come through the speakers, light and liquid. I wonder when he got the record, or who got it for him. Priscilla's hand is on my arm. "Don't I get to dance too?" she says. And so there we are, the four of us, drifting, shuffling around the dark floor. Priscilla's a good dancer, dainty and precise, likes to be led. We make a few fancy turns and then the music stops; the sound is out. We're all in the center of the room and Maria is standing in the hallway looking at us. My father walks over to speak to her. His back to us. Their voices rise and fall out of earshot. Catherine puts the record player away against the wall. Finally Priscilla says, "I'll drive her down." My father turns around. "That won't be necessary," he says. Maria has already vanished out the door.

Inside our room Catherine stood in her bare feet, half undressed, holding the blouse she'd taken off in one hand.

The only light came through the bathroom door ajar.

She turned in a slow pirouette, her pink skirt feathery and fluttering, her feet still moving to a dance step on the floorboards.

First I stood by the bed. Then I was standing close to her, more or less face to face. Her shoulders looked small and bony. The nipples on her bare breasts were dark and firm.

She let the blouse fall to the floor, reached up a hand to brush aside her hair, then dropped her arm again to her side; both arms at her sides.

I touched her hands with mine, fingertips pressed to fingertips.

I remember thinking her cheeks looked heavy—soft and heavy; and there was a drop or two of moisture on her upper lip.

"Fuck me, Tom," she said, almost a whisper.

She lay on the bed undressed. I went to lock the door.

"No one will come in," she said.

We coupled slickly, fiercely, breathing hard like athletes. I don't know that I'd ever seen her so excited, so beyond the usual limits. There was something wild and beautiful about it, a beauty of secrets, dangers, also simplicity.

I see Catherine's eyes open below me. Staring far out in front of her as at a distant shore. Oh, I don't mean she was uninvolved, detached! On the contrary she was all flesh and heat in the way she held me, in the way her body arched and her legs and knees pressed back against her chest.

"That's wonderful, baby," I said aloud at one moment, aware perhaps that I too was traveling in a new place.

"What's that?" she said as if my voice had woken her, although her eyes were already open.

"I said you were wonderful," I said.

"Say you want a baby," she hissed in my ear.

"I love you," I said.

"Say it," she said, her eyes closed, rocking up against me, rocking, rocking. "Say it, say it."

"I love you," I said again, which was God's truth. "I love you."

Afterward we lay under the single sheet, not spooned together as usual after lovemaking but on either side of the bed, our hands and fingers barely touching, like tendrils on two plants beneath the sea.

From the table in our room where I worked, you could (if so disposed) stare out the window at the smoky red hills that ran down the eastern flank of the valley almost a mile away: at the dark triangle of oak and pine halfway up one side, or the barren gash where part of a hill had slid down years ago, or the two old phone poles atop the nearest ridge or the big rock that loosely resembled (so somebody once insisted) an Indian's face in profile. Or else you could look right down below—here no more than a fifty-foot distance, the proverbial stone's throw—at the little green place (green from wild grasses on the bank and wild watercress at the water's edge) where the creek flowed by, past the old charred tree that always seemed about to topple but never did. A bend in the river, I guess you'd call it, if the creek had been a river. I can still see the two of them standing there that morning. Catherine in her khaki trousers, T-shirt, and running shoes. My father for some reason still wearing his bathrobe (more of an old-fashioned dressing gown;

dark blue and long like a floppy greatcoat) over trousers or pajamas, I don't know which. They were standing there in the hard bright eleven o'clock sunlight, just this side of the old tree. My father had the fishing rod in his hands. He'd turn sideways to the creek, whipping the rod back and forth, casting in the direction of the water. His form wasn't all that graceful, but as with riding he seemed to get the job done. The fact is I'd never seen him fly-cast before, never seen him with a fishing rod in his hands, so it rather surprised me to see him do it at all. After a few casts he handed the rod to Catherine. I could see him talking to her as she stood there next to him, whipping the line back and forth above her head, but I had no way of hearing what he was saying. It was all so lazy and yet definite. Her first cast was pretty; also her second. Then she dropped the fly right into one of the bushes near the water. I watched him go down the bank after it, clambering over the side in his bathrobe, feet and legs out of sight, the top of his white head bobbing amid the branches as he tried to disentangle the line. He got it too, bringing the freed line up from the creek like a prize. You could see where the lower part of his bathrobe was soaked from dragging in the water. Catherine had her head down as she reeled the line back in, although now and then she'd glance up and the sunlight would glitter in her hair. It was such a gentle scene. My father standing six feet away, arms folded across his chest, paternal. Then he grinned and for a second he looked just like one of those old Bedouin chiefs you used to see in photographs.

I saw you looking at me from the window," she said.
"I was looking at you cast," I said.
"It felt like you were saying goodbye," she said.
"Goodbye to him?"
"Goodbye to me."
"But it's not true," I said.
"Like you were on the deck of a ship waving goodbye to me."
"It's not true," I said.
"I don't know what's true anymore," she said.

With the sun on our backs we were riding up in the red hills, his black horse, my brown horse, moving along in tandem at a brisk walk. Red dirt. Red rocks. Scrub oak and piñon here and there. "You want to ride some fence?" he'd said to me earlier. I hadn't ridden with him since that time we jumped the ditches a week ago. "Sure," I said, figuring he wanted me to do it on my own, but it turned out he meant both of us. We were looking for downed wire or a break in the fence, whatever it was that had put a six-inch gash on the foreleg of one of the mares. We started just above the ranch to the right and then went up into the hills following the old wire fence straight across, an easy job except when it dipped down into arroyos.

"What makes you think it's out this way," I said, making conversation.

"Because I asked Billy Gaines to check it," he said, "and I know he's too fucking lazy to go out this far."

He was silent most of the way out, sitting his horse

stiff and upright. No windbreaker this time; an old work shirt on his broad back. He was riding well too, large in the saddle as always, but poised and easy, more like a rancher than a general. We went down into an arroyo littered with shards of broken green glass, then up again. The fence ran along beside us, unbroken, though I wasn't thinking much about the fence and didn't think he was either.

I kept wanting to ask him questions, those dumb break-the-silence questions: Hey, how are you? How was your day? Are you going to win another Oscar at seventy-two? But I knew he didn't want to answer them so I kept silent too. Besides I was having a good time riding. After a week of taking Toby out on my own, he was leaner and stronger, more spring to his step, more like a mountain horse than a pudding, and I was in better shape myself. I trotted up next to the old man. "Toby's lost a bit of weight, don't you think?"

He was riding along, hat low on his forehead, eyes straight in front of him. At first he didn't say anything; then he said, "They all cost too fucking much to keep."

Please turn your head, I thought. Turn your head and look at the horse. Look at me. "All I'm saying is if you exercise him, he's a pretty good horse."

Now he looked at me. "You know a lot about horses, do you?"

"I know a little," I said. But then he turned his head away again, almost out of boredom so it seemed, and we rode on side by side in silence. You're such a big fucking deal, I thought, how come you can't ever give any of it away, how come you can't just give a little of that away? Out of the corner of my eye I watched him there, tall in the saddle as the saying goes, motionless, solid, looking neither to the right or left but like an old eagle presumably seeing everything.

We came scrambling up out of another arroyo onto a long stretch of flat ground when one of the horses saw something, or thought it saw something, and both bounded ahead, loping across the red dirt for the sheer hell of it. He soon pulled his horse up and I did too, but as we were standing there I suddenly said, "You want to run?"

He was staring away from the fence, down the hill, down past the old irrigation ditch to where a half dozen horses were grazing about a mile away. He looked back at me. "Is that what you want to do?" he said.

"Sure thing," I said, feeling not only young but young and capable, feeling for the first time since I'd been back that I could probably take him.

And so we ran our horses across the powdery red dirt, across the top of the red hills, our animals snorting, pounding along parallel to the fence, the warm air blowing in our faces, stones and dirt flying up behind us. There was a real joy to it, a feeling of exhilaration. I knew I was riding well this time, stronger and better than I had as a kid. For a whole long moment, careening across the red dirt, I felt I could do anything I wanted to on a horse—leap ditches, jump pipes, soar above the hillside. I was riding a little ahead of the old man now and I could see him hunched forward, no longer quite so upright and solid, elbows flying wider, hands higher, close to his belly. Hey, I can beat you! I thought. I can beat you at one of your crazy games! In front of us, about a quarter mile away, was a grove of scrub oak; nothing much it looked like at a distance. I meant to stop old Toby before we got there, before we reached the trees, but Toby didn't stop or maybe I didn't try hard enough. We all went flying into the grove—more than a grove it was, more than a few trees. A small wood like the other. Downed timber underfoot. We didn't take it at a gallop but we took it at a very fast lope and there were times I was certain that something very terrible was about to happen to one of us, or both of us—a branch too low, a fallen tree! But nothing happened. We made it through. I stopped Toby just beyond the trees on the far side.

The first thing I noticed was that the old man had lost his hat. "You okay?" I said.

"Why did you stop?" he said brusquely. His shirt was wet and he was breathing hard.

"You want your hat?" I said. I was thinking, why can't you once just give me something, why couldn't you once say, "Tom, you handled that pretty well . . ."

"Never mind the fucking hat," he said. "Why did you stop?"

"I just stopped," I said.

"Well, we're here to ride some fence," he said, and off we started, following the fence line at a trot.

Beyond the next gully the fence angled downhill to the left, down toward lower ground, across the irrigation ditch, then over toward a grove of aspen in the distance where the old cabin used to be. The Darby cabin was its official name, after a legendary prospector who supposedly lived there years ago, but I always thought of it as Charlie's cabin because he used to keep a bedroll there in the summer months, sleeping out on warm nights, so he said, drinking blackberry brandy and howling at the moon.

I saw the grove of aspen but not the cabin.

"Where's the cabin?" I said.

The old man didn't say anything. I figured I must have remembered the wrong grove of aspen. But we came up a rise in the ground, looking down on the aspen grove, and there where the cabin once stood was nothing but a jumble of planks and timber on the ground.

"Jesus, what happened?" I said.

The old man still didn't say anything. I rode up beside him. "What happened to the Darby cabin?" I said.

"It burned down," he said.

Old planks and timber lying about. Pieces of tin roof. There were signs of a fire on the ground but most of the wood looked unburned.

"What kind of fire?" I said.

"How in hell should I know what kind of fire?" he said. "Are you riding fence or on a sightseeing tour?"

We went along the flat for a while, then climbed again. Piñon and cactus. Sagebrush and glistening rock. I knew we'd never find a break in the fence, at least not there, but then the old man stopped next to a red rock. "What do you see?" I said because I couldn't see anything, just the empty terrain and the fence threading up and down the arroyos. The old man got off his horse, started to walk forward, and then I saw it too. In a stretch down in one of the arroyos, there was a dead animal caught in the wire. A deer it looked like, that had lost its footing or got scared and had pulled a whole section of barbed-wire fence apart before dying there. All that was left of it, after the birds and the coyotes, was a sad-looking hide, some mangy bones, and a couple of hooves. We climbed down and restrung the loose wire as best we could and put what we couldn't restring out of harm's way.

"That's an awful way to die," I said as we came back out of the arroyo.

"You think there's a good way?" he said, his face covered in sweat, his eyes red and rheumy from the wind and dust.

We started back across the hills, with the horses moving slowly in the heat. I was riding out front when we came to a fork in the trail: the right-hand path taking us back the way we came—safe, sure, and uncomplicated; the left-hand fork leading briefly down through a willow grove as I remembered it, then steeply up again, above the hills, around the back of a piny mountain—a shortcut I suppose you'd call it; a nervy route, not meant for tourists.

"Let's go left," I said.

He nodded, which might have meant anything, including yes.

We took our horses down, over large smooth stones;

then past willows, gray with dirt; then up a gravelly trail, more of a game trail really, climbing the mountainside—steep and narrow; steeper than I remembered it.

Above us on a ledge were three pine trees standing in a row, as if they'd been planted there.

The image of the deer (and of death) had almost vanished from my mind. Instead I was caught up in the excitement of the moment, as well as the precariousness of the place I'd taken us to.

Out in front on Toby, I made my way slowly across the flank of the mountain. The downhill slope on our left was as steep as a ski jump. "Don't slip, Toby, don't slip," I muttered, but I didn't think he would. I looked back over my shoulder at the old man. He was plodding forward on the black horse, head down, picking his way cautiously. I thought, what happens if his horse slips? "Let's keep moving!" he barked from behind.

In due course the trail narrowed even more, and the terrain turned to crumbly stone. Both animals were making their way now with a kind of harrowing daintiness, only a step at a time, the loose stones tumbling down the hill to the rocky bottom. Then I came around a curve and the trail stopped altogether, ending abruptly in a huge pile of rocks left by a rockslide. There was no going higher, no going forward, no room to turn around and go back. So I thought, let's do it, let's go down. I urged Toby to take a tentative step down the incline, one foot, two feet; then he slipped. This is crazy, I thought. The damned horses are going to kill themselves. I turned Toby sideways to the hill and dismounted.

"What are you doing?" the old man called.

"I don't want the horses to hurt themselves," I said, taking Toby by the reins and trying to lead him down the hill. Underfoot were more loose stones and red sand. "Easy, Toby, easy," I said, though my own boots were slipping more than he was. Behind me I noticed the old man still on his horse, starting down the side of the hill, horse and rider at such a dangerous angle that I thought one or both of them must surely fall, and looked away, back to my own problems. Toby's front legs were braced, his back legs were sliding. I tried to guide him forward where I thought the slope might be firmer, but it was all pretty soft, and difficult for either of us to find purchase on it. Toby took a step down, then two steps, then started to slip. My own feet were sliding then; Toby's wild eyes were just over my shoulder. I tried to turn him left, away from a bad spot, but then he turned too much, came stumbling forward, sliding, slipping right at me, started to fall, both front knees down. I leapt out of the way, falling myself, as Toby came crashing down where I'd been standing, then slid, legs flailing, a sickening mess of horse, saddle, and dust, at least twenty feet down the slope. I ran after him, trying to hold him on the ledge where he'd stopped, trying to get him to rise, which was no easy matter.

"Loop your reins around the horn!" my father yelled. I looked up and there he was, over to the right, still astride the black horse, sidling down the hill (steep as a ski run, as I said), just riding the horse down, a slip here, a little sliding there, sand and loose stones cascading around them, not elegant maybe but doing it, damn unbelievably doing it.

After several false tries, Toby got to his feet. I took the reins and looped them around the saddle horn.

"Walk behind him!" my father called from below, still riding the black horse down.

I walked behind Toby, stumbling and slipping in front of me, one leg limping badly it seemed to me, his saddle all askew, his flanks covered with red dust. When we reached the flat ground at the bottom, my father was sitting there on his horse waiting for us, as erect in the saddle as when we'd started. I couldn't look at him, could barely look at Toby, who was hobbling around on his game foot.

"Next time stay mounted," he said.

"Thanks, I will," I said.

"Stay mounted or walk behind him."

"You're pretty big with the advice, aren't you?" I said.

"I didn't tell you to get off the horse," he said.

"You didn't tell me a fucking thing," I said. "You never did and you never will. We could have both slid to the bottom of that fucking hill."

"But we both didn't," he said. "Can you ride him?"

"Of course I can't ride him," I said.

"Then you'd better walk," he said.

"Go fuck yourself," I said, but he was already turned about and moving off, and I was following on foot, leading Toby. We stayed in that order of procession all the way back, with him two or three hundred yards in front and me and Toby bringing up the rear. You bastard, I thought. You cold bastard. I didn't know which was worse, what had happened on the slope or my disintegrating into an adolescent. Stop it, I said to myself, stop it, stop it. Stay cool. And so I stayed as cool as I could manage, my feet blistering in my boots, my legs aching from the fall (though not as badly as Toby's), all the way back across the fields below the ranch, down past the willows and the winding creek, and finally into the corral. My father was there ten minutes ahead of us and was unsaddled by the time I appeared. Catherine was also there waiting, I didn't know for whom, standing by herself in a far corner of the corral, shielding her eyes from the sun. None of us spoke. My father took a brush and brushed something off the back of the black horse, then disappeared inside the barn. I unsaddled Toby and took a look at his foot. "I'm sorry, Toby," I said foolishly and let him limp out into the pasture. And then I'm afraid I went up the hill toward the house without a backward glance.

Time kept slipping by in the haze and heat. African mornings, yellow and flat, the sun straight overhead, no shadows on the ground. Only the mountains faraway, dark and cool: an ancient animal stretched across the earth. Each day part of me wanted to leave the ranch, to be somewhere else, couldn't bear (so I thought) to stay another moment in this barren, beautiful kingdom—my father's kingdom under my father's rule. At the same time I knew we'd be heading out of there before too long, back to New York, and I was secretly scared to go. I couldn't imagine life in either place.

Five days before the time set for our departure, Donald Newcome arrived for a long weekend—my father's screenwriter and collaborator on *Rio Rigo*. Before his arrival I watched Maria trot back and forth with little guest towels and flowery boxes of Kleenex to the other guest room on the second floor. Even my father expressed a housekeeperly interest. "Let's make sure he's got some soap in there!" I heard him call. "Let's make sure there aren't any goddamn beetles in that closet!" I wondered if any such preparations had preceded our arrival and thought it unlikely; at any rate there were always beetles everywhere, especially in the closets.

I was determined to like Newcome or at least get on with him, but we met inauspiciously. I was down at the barn rubbing ointment on Toby's slowly mending foot when he arrived, ferried in by Billy Gaines from the Albuquerque airport, and my first glimpse of him was from an upstairs window where I was changing: my father and this young man walking together beneath the trees in back of the house. They weren't exactly arm in arm but it somehow seemed like it. The old man's head was bent low as if he was deep in conversation, or even listening for a change, and there was a comradely, tender air to their pacing that gave the impression they'd been partners all their lives. When I came downstairs Newcome was standing alone in the living room. "You must be Tom," he said, extending a hand to greet me as if I were the guest and he the host. In some ways he was the youngest man I'd ever seen. His actual age I guessed to be about thirty—conceivably younger—but there was something virginal in his smooth tanned face (smooth, one felt, despite the faint shadow of a beginner's beard), his soft careful hair, in his new bluejeans and new Levi jacket and loafers, in his dogged show of confidence. "You live here too?" he said, drifting in the direction of the little porch outside, thus compelling me to follow him as if I were being shown about the house. "No," I said, thinking to be curt. But Newcome hadn't noticed. "I live in LAX," he said. "That's short for L.A." Then he waved his hand in the general direction of the outdoors. "But I can really get off on this." My father's heavy footfall sounded across the floorboards of the living room behind us. "Newcome!" he bellowed. "Donald Newcome!" And, "Where in hell is he?" Newcome himself remained surprisingly unruffled throughout this outburst, though he ceased from contemplating the landscape and was turning around as my father hove into view in the doorway. "Ah, Donald!" my father said, with an expression of such radiant affability that I thought he might be about to add, "Quel plaisir!" But instead he caught sight of me off to one side. "Goddamit, Tom, we've got work to do," he said crossly, implying either that the whole concept of serious work was alien to me, or else that I'd been trying to lead his youthful co-worker astray. "Don't let me keep you from anything," I said to Newcome. "You weren't keeping me," he said. "Besides, I always enjoy a break in the routine." And off they marched, the two collaborators, Newcome scuffling along behind my father, trying so it seemed to keep one of his new loafers from falling off his foot.

At dinner, I suppose for the edification of Newcome, my father told us about the filming of *Dakar*. "Worse fucking mess I ever was involved with," he said. "Hell, we could have done it easy on the lot at Metro. Or at one of the big outfits like Shepperton in England. But, no sir, Jimmy Wildman says it has to be a location picture in Africa. A location picture! Hell, I think he just wanted to show off to everyone that he could be a bloody global producer like Zanuck. So, first we move everyone to Dakar which is just an awful place. But then there's some kind of snafu with the French Navy—Monsieur le Admiral not getting his ten percent—and so we pick up and move along the coast to Rabat, which is even worse. I'm telling you, one of the stinkholes of the world. Heat and fucking flies and those pissant Arabs stealing your shoes while you're standing in them. It got so hot you could fry eggs on the cameras by midday so we used to set up before dawn—Christ, in the middle of the goddamn night—and try to finish shooting by noon. The rest of the time there wasn't much to do but drink. I think just about everyone in the cast was either drunk or sick the whole time we were there."

"Even Nigel Beecham?" said Newcome in an awed voice.

"Nigel Beecham my ass," my father said. "Goddamn fruitcake arrived at the airport with two whole cases of some killer Dutch gin, a valet carrying a flyswatter—strangest guy I ever saw—and two little Greek boys of fourteen he introduced to everyone as his nephews. I'm telling you the place was a fucking madhouse. Johnny Grahame actually went out of his mind one day. They found him in the closet in his hotel room—our bloody star sitting buck-naked on the floor of his closet. We pulled him out and got some clothes on him—hell, I thought he was only drunk—but then he hid under the bed and started tearing his clothes off again. There wasn't anything to do but wait it out. One time I even found him sitting on the floor of *my* closet. 'Goddamit, go and sit on the floor of your own fucking closet,' I said to him. He was like that for a whole week, but then he snapped out of it and was just as friendly and cooperative as could be for the rest of the movie. Johnny was really a very decent guy. Very courageous. You know, he was decorated in the war. He flew bombers or something with the Canadian Air Force. But Jesus he was an awful fool with women."

"That's such a funny expression," said Catherine. "A fool with women."

"For a while after the war he was married to a gal

called Velma," my father said. "Velma-with-a-V is what everybody called her. I guess she didn't like people calling her Thelma, so the first thing she always said to anyone she met was, 'It's Velma with a V,' and naturally that's what we all called her. I think she'd been one of Billy Rose's show girls, at least for a couple of weeks. She had a good figure all right, but one of those sharp little faces and a voice you could wake chickens with. She once told me her ambition was to play opposite Johnny in a remake of *Robin Hood*. 'Won't he look terrific swinging on those vines and wrestling with the animals,' she said. 'You're thinking of Tarzan,' I said. 'Oh, I hate Tarzan,' she said. 'All he ever cared about was those faggot apes.' I remember she and Johnny would give these parties —bottles of Canadian whiskey, I guess because he was Canadian, and bowls of avocado spread. And card playing—canasta. Jesus, I never could stand canasta."

"Did he love her?" Catherine said.

"Johnny loved every girl he married," my father said. "After Velma-with-a-V there was a big English dame called Margot. She was crazy about gardening, but she wouldn't go outside the house during the day because she was afraid the California sun would ruin her complexion. So she had Johnny string lights all around the house and she did her gardening at night. Christ, I never knew any dame who could talk as much about mulch and compost as Margot could. But she had a younger sister Eve who was something else —a real knockout, but shy like a young Audrey Hepburn. Always kept to herself. The Lady Eve we used to call her, after the movie." My father poured some more wine in his glass and took a sip. "The funny thing is I never had much to do with Evie out in Hollywood," he said, "but one time I ran into her back East. By then I think she was married to this banking guy from Baltimore—Thompson or Timpson. I was out at this party in one of those big Long Island houses. You know, a lot of fancy dancing and drinking; everybody bored out of their socks. I saw her across the room standing next to these guys, Long Island guys talking about the stock market or their golf games. Finally she walks over to me. 'I saw you looking at me,' she said. 'Well, it's a free country,' I said. 'What were you thinking when you were looking at me?' she said. 'A penny for your thoughts.' I always hated it when dames said that to me—a penny for your thoughts—but there was something different about Evie, so I said, 'If you want to know, I was thinking you were probably the best lay in the room.' I didn't know if she was going to slap my face or not. She was looking at me so quiet and serious. But then she said, 'Well, if you're interested'—that's what she said—'if you're interested I think I know where I can find the keys to the pool house.' "

"Sam, you're shameless!" Catherine said, with a quick smile.

"Damn right I'm shameless," he said. "Goddamnedest pool house you ever saw." He turned to Newcome. "What say, Donald?"

"You know, I think I studied *The Lady Eve* in film school," Newcome said.

"Good man," my father said, pushing his chair back from the table and standing up. "Let's do some work."

Questions. Who was the woman he'd brought to that party on Long Island, who must have waited, patiently or not so patiently, while he fucked shy Lady Eve in the fabulous pool house? Who was the long-haired woman in my dream? Or did both women only exist in dreams?

But I had no more dreams to remember, and didn't sleep much either until just before dawn. The night as blank and restless as a long plane trip. In the morning I made myself sit at my table upstairs—a charade of discipline and professionalism—while staring at my notes and manuscript like some advertising copywriter who has taken a cabin in Vermont to write "his novel" only to find that the literary impulse has abandoned him. For the first time in my working life even the simplest sentence wouldn't form itself in my mind, or on the page, and when one did it made no sense. The very act of writing seemed unimportant, a waste of time. Did someone like Newcome, for example, care about words, magazine articles, books—text is probably what he called it—and who could blame him if he didn't in this glorious era of film, pictures, movies, the almighty screen? Downstairs, in fact, sandwiched between endless phone calls about "the deal" and a visit from Ernie of Ernie's Propane, he and my father could be heard engaged in the creative process, sometimes (as if for my benefit) in the hallway right beneath the stairs.

"I don't think we need that locomotive sequence, Donald," my father was saying.

"I thought a train might give us, you know, another dimension," Newcome said.

"It's not a fucking train picture," my father said.

"Okay, no train," Newcome said. "Strike pages 32 to 33 . . ."

Later Catherine came in the room, out of breath as if she'd been running. "Oh, hi," she said.

"You look surprised," I said, I suppose because her eyes had jumped a little when she saw me there.

"I didn't want to disturb you," she said, taking off her T-shirt and throwing it on the bed.

"You didn't disturb me," I said.

"I'm going to the shopping center," she said, slipping on a clean polo shirt over her bare breasts. "Do you want anything?"

"No, thanks," I said.

"Razor blades?" she said, looking in the mirror, doing something to her eyes. "Shaving cream?"

"Nothing, thanks," I said. "But you better put some gas in the car."

"Actually I'm going in the truck," she said.

"The truck?"

"Sam's taking me," she said. She stood in front of the dresser brushing out her hair, then tied on the red headband, then turned around. "You don't mind, do you?"

"No," I said.

"You're sure?"

"I'm sure."

She picked up her wallet, then paused. "If you'd rather I didn't," she said.

"No, it's fine," I said.

"Well, I have to run," she said, standing before me with a clear, bright look on her face, her nipples like little berries under the cotton shirt. "Work hard and get lots of writing done and maybe we can do something together when I get back." She smiled like a young girl, planted a kiss on my lips, stepped back, and darted out the corridor and down the stairs.

The strangest thing is that I was glad to see her go. I remember even thinking that with *him* out of the house—his voice and his boots and his banging around—I might be able to get something done for a change. But it didn't work that way and in a while I went downstairs myself and was standing dumbly by the kitchen sink when Newcome walked in.

"What's the access code here anyway?" he said.

"One-three," I said.

"One-*three*?" he said. "I never heard of one-*three* before." He went out again in the direction of my father's study.

Since it was around lunchtime I found a can of tuna in one of the cupboards and opened it with a thought to fixing myself some tuna salad, but then lost interest in the salad part and sat down at the kitchen table with fork and can and yesterday's Albuquerque newspaper.

Newcome reappeared. "He's getting a haircut," he said.

"Who?" I said.

"Herb Prochnow," he said. "Mr. Powerful. I thought guys like that had the barber come to their office." He eyed my can of tuna. "You on some kind of special diet?"

"I don't think so," I said.

Newcome opened the door of the fridge and studied the interior as if it were a major painting. "Who eats the Jell-O?" he said.

"My father," I said, taking a guess.

Newcome removed two eggs, an aged tomato, an equally veteran green pepper, some stalks of celery, and God knows what else and put them all on the counter, and then started rummaging around in the cupboards for little jars of spices.

"I don't think this dill is fresh," he said, sniffing the contents of a green bottle.

"I'll tell Maria," I said.

"Tell her to try the gourmet department where she shops," he said. "All the supermarkets have a gourmet department now."

"I'll do that," I said.

I continued reading the paper while Newcome clattered about beside the stove, now with skillet, now with two skillets, plus much chopping and sprinkling and stirring and serious chef-like behavior.

"You wrote that book about Alaska and the Northwest," Newcome said above the sound of sizzling.

"*Northwest Territories*," I said. "Actually it's more about Hudson's Bay."

"That's it, Hudson's Bay," he said. "I brought it

with me on vacation to Baja and just about finished it. But then my girlfriend ran off and she took it with her." With a flourish of spoons and spatulas, Newcome now extracted what seemed to be an omelet from one of the skillets, placed it tenderly on a plate, poured something over it from the other skillet, produced knife and fork, then paper napkin, then salt and pepper, then bottle of ketchup, and sat himself down opposite me at the kitchen table. "I always make it a point to eat a hot lunch," he said.

"That's a good idea," I said.

"Best thing for the digestion," he said. "A hot lunch settles you down. I think it expands the intestines, or maybe it contracts them. Anyway, I got into the habit at film school and just sort of kept it up."

Newcome ate in careful, measured mouthfuls, keeping his eyes for the most part on his plate, though now and then glancing out the window on his left as if he were on a train looking out at the passing scenery.

"This is some place," he said, "but you know somehow I expected more trees."

"Farther north," I said.

Newcome nodded in agreement. "I get you," he said. "All the same I expected more trees." He ate for a while more in silence, then looked over at me with the gravest of expressions. "Imagine being Sam Avery's son! Growing up as Sam Avery's son! It really blows my mind just thinking about it."

"Sometimes it's had the same effect on me," I said.

"You know, my parents aren't anybody," Newcome said. "They aren't even creative. My dad's in the rug-shampooing business in Buffalo, New York, although he was actually trained in construction. He was a Seabee in the Korean War—pontoon bridges and shit like that. But I guess they didn't need pontoon bridges after the war, at least not in Buffalo. Now you could say he's pretty well trained in rug shampooing." After taking the last bite of the omelet, Newcome arranged his knife and fork together in the middle of his plate. "How come you never wrote a screenplay?" he said.

"I just never did," I said.

"With Sam Avery as your old man you could get in to see any agent in Hollywood," he said. "You could just walk right in. You'd have access."

"I'm sure you're right," I said.

"You think access isn't important?" he said. "Access is everything. Listen, Sam Avery's still a very big man in this business. People pay a lot of attention to him."

"I hope so," I said.

"You'd better believe it," Newcome said, getting to his feet. "Well, that *Northwest Territories* was a good book. I enjoyed reading it even if I didn't get to the last part."

"Thanks," I said.

"It won some kind of an award, didn't it?" he said.

"Something called the Jennings Medal," I said.

"Yeah, my girlfriend said it won some kind of an award," he said, heading for the door. "Well, back on the trail of Herb Prochnow."

With Newcome gone, I looked at my watch. A quarter to two. Catherine should be back from town by two o'clock. I threw out my tuna can and cleaned up after Newcome's lunch, feeling no special ill will toward him for having left his litter behind, but rather as if I were the resident parent picking up after the children.

The screen door banged and Maria entered from the rear carrying a grocery bag. "I do that," she said.

"It's okay," I said. "I'm nearly finished." But I wasn't anywhere near finished so I stepped aside.

"Your wife not clean up?" she said, standing at the sink.

"This is Mr. Newcome's stuff," I said.

Maria started to plunge the remaining lunch gear into soapy water. Broad shoulders under her cotton smock.

"Anyway, Catherine picks up after herself," I said —the loyal husband.

With one hand holding a skillet, she scoured it with a vigorous sweeping motion of her thick arm.

"She and my father drove into town," I said.

Maria put the skillet down and turned around. "Into town?" she said. "Where into town?"

"The shopping center," I said. "I guess the drugstore."

"She should stay here and cook you lunch," she said. "She never cooks you lunch."

"That's not true," I said.

I don't know whether Maria dropped the skillet or banged it on the counter. "It *is* true!" she said with surprising vehemence. "I see it!" Her eyes black and furious. Then she turned around and started to run fresh water in the sink.

"I know you don't mean that, Maria," I said.

"Mr. Thomas Avery," she said, though in a much softer voice and not really to me. She pronounced my first name in the Spanish manner: Tomás.

How many times have I heard someone say, "I'm no good at waiting!" Often with the appearance of regret but really as a boast. As if to say, I'm not the kind of person that gets pushed around by Time. And how I envy them—those people who think they can push Time around. For my part, I've always been good at waiting. Perhaps too good at it. It's probably one of the by-products or side effects of having a famous parent. Or else of having parents who aren't too happily married. Or maybe it's just part of my nature, my temperament. I'm good at waiting. At being alone. I'm adept, even expert you might say, at not flying off the handle, not being impatient, not rushing about or jumping up and down, not kicking at the waves like King Canute trying to bully back the tides. Not being like my father. No, I handle waiting well. I engage in modest tasks, concentrate on little things. The point is not to be too passive. The point is to let Time do what it wants. That afternoon, for example, I took a walk down past the barn, across the fields. I noted leaves on the willow branches. Blackbirds on the fence. I counted stones in the stream. Two-thirty. Three o'clock. Then three-thirty. I was not unhappy. Doubtless that's a virtue of being on one's own a lot while growing up. If anything, I think I was happy that they were happy. Back upstairs in our room I was lying on the bed for a moment, for not at all long, not even dozing, when I heard the sound of the pickup in the driveway. Four o'clock. The front door opening, closing. My father's heavy footfall downstairs in the hallway.

I was back sitting at my worktable when Catherine came in the door. Came bursting in the door. Then closed it quietly behind her. "Hi," she said. Her cheeks red from the sun. Her eyes very bright. "Are you still working?" She carried two small paper parcels in her hand, presumably the reason for the expedition.

"In a manner of speaking," I said.

She put the parcels on the dresser top. "I'm sorry we're so late," she said. She shook out her hair as if shaking out dust.

"That's okay," I said.

"We had lunch at a chili place near the highway," she said.

"Until four o'clock?" I said.

"You're mad," she said. Suddenly hurt. Staring at me. "Please don't be mad."

"I'm not mad," I said.

She smiled. "Please don't be," she said. "I had such a good time. Then afterward we drove up into the hills to this old mission church. You must have seen it."

"Yes," I said.

"It was so beautiful," she said. "So simple and beautiful. Those old stone walls." She took a few steps toward me. Standing maybe five feet away. "It felt so free up there in the hills," she said. She was looking at me with these bright eyes of hers, brighter than I'd seen them in days, and all the while I was looking at her, though I had the feeling that neither of us could see the other with any clarity. She stepped closer, sat down on my knees, first sideways, then astride them, like riding a horse, her legs on either side of mine. "Touch me," she said quietly.

"Touch you?" I said.

Her face serious, without expression; without known expression. "Please touch me," she said.

I raised my hand to the side of her face. Her cheek unexpectedly cool and damp. Wordlessly, with both her hands, she raised the bottom of her cotton shirt up and over her belly, past her breasts. Above her bare breasts. My hand still on her cheek. She took my hand then, brought it to her breasts, one breast and then the other. Cool also. Dry not damp. My hand dry on her skin. Palm pressed against firm nipple.

She stood up, took off her shirt. "Aren't you going to get undressed?" she said. Her clothes scattering on the floor.

Taking off my own clothes. Shoes and socks. Shirt and trousers on the chair. I felt, we're in a strange place here. Strangers in a strange place. Catherine lying on the bed in white underpants. She gives a little wriggle, shucks them off. I lie down beside her, next to her, close to her, waiting to feel something. "Don't you want to kiss me?" she said.

I kissed her, our mouths opening, our tongues tangling. I could feel liquid sensations begin to run up my limbs but without warmth or urgency; they faded away as soon as they neared my groin.

"What's the matter?" she said after a while.

"Nothing," I said.

"Don't you like me?" she said.

"Yes, I like you," I said. But all I could feel was an absence of feeling, an emptiness as heavy and palpable as a weight.

Catherine sat up beside me, fondling my limp cock in her hand, then bent down, pressing her lips against it, then engulfed it with open mouth. Eyes closed, tight-closed. Her face set in a kind of grin; an imitation of a grin. The truth is I'd never felt her mouth like that before, so devouring and so detached; a devourment beyond love and even hunger. She raised her head. "Tell me what I'm doing wrong?" she said.

"It's not you," I said.

"What is it?" she said.

"It's me," I said.

She lay beside me holding my cock in her hand, slowly rubbing it, rubbing it up and down. "You have to tell me what to do," she said. Intense and serious, like a child.

"Anything," I said.

"You have to tell me!" she said.

"Anything you want," I said. "Or nothing."

"Not *anything* or *nothing*!" she said. I felt her close to tears; a new kind of tears. "*Tell* me!"

Then gradually, with the motion of her hand, I began to stiffen, though I could tell it was more from friction than from libido. She was lying down next to me, face close to mine, skin to skin, eyes closed. "I know you love me," she said.

"Of course I love you," I said.

"And you didn't mind my being with him?" she said, her voice a whisper.

"No, I didn't mind," I said.

Her lips nibbling on mine. Stroking me with her hand. "I know you didn't mind," she said. Voice so soft I can barely hear it. "I think you like it when I'm with him. Don't you?" Soft and faraway as in a dream.

"I don't know," I said.

"I can see it on your face sometimes," she said. Eyes closed. Lips against my ear. She moved on top of me, my cock between us, harder but not hard enough; not hard enough inside. Fumbling, insistent, eyes still closed, she pressed me into her, mounted me as they say. Riding me. Awkward, strange. I prayed that it would work, would last, but I knew it wouldn't. "Come on, Tommy," she said, off in her dream, off in some other world. "Yes, yes," she said. But I could feel myself softening, lessening, going, going . . . gone.

Her eyes opened. "What's *wrong*?" she said. Awake and lost. "What's *wrong*?"

"I don't know," I said.

"You don't love me," she said.

"I do love you," I said.

"No, you don't love me," she said. "Nobody ever loved me." She was lying on her side, her back to me, her eyes staring at the wall. "I felt so free this afternoon up in the hills," she said. Then she got up from the bed, picked up her clothes, went into the bathroom. I could hear the bath running, for close to twenty minutes it seemed like. She came out naked, silent, holding a towel against her, dressed quickly. "I'll see you downstairs," she said.

I felt for the first time that I'd somehow lost Catherine, almost in the literal sense of the word, as if we'd been journeying together through the proverbial dark wood (in bright Southwestern sunlight!) —through some dream kingdom—and now she was no longer with me, at my side; as if "my" Catherine had in fact disappeared, vanished from sight, supplanted by this other Catherine I saw that evening: her face beautiful, frozen, austere, like porcelain, like a mask. But if I'd lost her, or we'd lost each other, there was something about the transaction that was clearly more and less than loss. There was a gain I couldn't put my finger on but I could sense, in my new calm as well as hers. For we were both strangely peaceful in our own ways, in our own orbits, not at all like tense or impatient lovers straining to keep back an argument. I watched her with my father and I suppose I could have felt sadness, anger, jealousy that she so enjoyed his company, and he hers. But the truth is I felt so moved by it. I felt he made things safe for her in ways I couldn't; and that she made things safe for him, in ways I also couldn't.

Ladies and gentlemen, I think maybe we can go the distance with *Rio Rigo*," he was saying. There were times he looked as wild and fierce as an old sea captain.

"What do you mean, go the distance?" Catherine said. A snow princess with suntanned arms and legs; again in her pink skirt.

"He means that if we get the deal we want," said Newcome in his best junior-executive manner, "then we start shooting in the fall, and release next summer, and then we can be up for an Oscar the following spring."

"Oh, Sam, an Oscar!" Catherine said.

"I can feel it here," he said, his eyes glittering like Ahab's, patting his hard sea captain's belly.

I said, "Did you actually ever read any of my books?"

"I got a couple of 'em around somewhere," he said. "I think somebody sent me two of the things in the mail."

"I sent them to you," I said. "But did you read them?"

"You mean all the way through?" he said.

"Well, that's the way they were written," I said. "I guess I thought *Northwest Territories* might interest you."

"Very fancy writing," he said.

"Thanks," I said.

"Must be hard work writing all those long sentences," he said.

"Then you didn't read them?" I said.

"Jesus, I didn't say I didn't read 'em," he said. "I just said I didn't finish 'em."

My father and Catherine playing backgammon after dinner. He with brandy and cigar, she with coffee, both in silence.

Newcome on the couch, correcting script pages. "I think I may be coming down with a cold," he said.

"Then go to bed," my father said curtly.

"It's not really a cold," he said. "It's more like a sore throat. But I don't want it to get down into the chest. If it gets down in the chest—"

"Take some brandy and go to bed," my father said.

Newcome leaned back, closing his eyes. "I think I may do that," he said.

"Do it," my father said.

"Well, I guess I'll be going to bed," Newcome said, getting to his feet.

Good nights were exchanged. Catherine and my father continued at their game, or games. Now and then he'd get up and light another cigar or pour himself some more brandy; in a while he brought Catherine a glass of brandy, which she sipped. I sat on the couch reading one of my research books, *Occupational Safety*, by a team of subliterate professors at a Texas university. Had another beer. Moved to a chair. Back to the couch. Finally had enough of book and beer and couch, got to my feet too. "I'm turning in," I said.

"Good night," my father said, not looking up.

"I'll be up after this game," Catherine said, sipping her brandy. She picked up the tumbler and rolled the dice.

Upstairs in our room. The night black beyond the window. No wind. Newcome down the corridor moving in his room. Then silence. I opened the window wider, letting in a denser silence from outside. Lay under the covers. The sheets cold, the bed cold. Got up to get a blanket. Got up to get my book and tried to read. An hour later I put on my robe and went downstairs.

Catherine and my father were still at the backgammon table. I heard him say something in a low rumbly voice; then she laughed, a sudden peal of laughter.

"You're still playing?" I said, coming up beside her.

"Yes," she said, neither friendly nor unfriendly. "Is it all right?"

"I guess so," I said. "It's pretty late."

"What's the matter, you got a cold too?" he said.

"No," I said.

"You got a problem?" he said.

"No," I said.

"I'll be up soon," Catherine said.

"Come on, it's your move," he said. "This is championship play."

Catherine rolled the dice and moved her counters. She had a studious, schoolgirl look to her when she played; deliberate and serious. My father, on the other hand, never appeared to be studying the board, but once he rolled he marched his counters swiftly, noisily, like an assault.

"Will you come up after this game?" I said.

"Why are you doing this?" she said. "I'll be up when we're done."

"When you're done?" I said.

"Didn't you hear the lady?" my father said.

"Don't you trust me?" she said. Her new voice. Not even a real question.

"Yes," I said, and went back upstairs, hearing the faint clink of counters as I walked down the corridor to our room and bed. The night was so very quiet: still no wind, no breeze, no air moving; no branches scraping on the roof. I was asleep but half woke up when Catherine came in at last. Undressed in the bathroom. Bare feet across the floor. A shadow in a dark room. Slipping coolly into bed on the far side. Night and silence.

"Who's taking me to the airport anyway?" Newcome said.

"I'm taking you," I said.

The weather changed. You could feel it changing first high above the earth. The sky still blue, but the haze suddenly gone from the valley and much of the heat too. Miles overhead, the wispy cirrus clouds were streaked across the sky, and despite the brightness of the sun—a sort of fever glare—there was something crisp, almost chill, in the air. Like on those days right after Labor Day when summer vanishes—vanishes overnight—and people start to think of fall and falling leaves and death: the death of the year.

My father walking with Catherine across the grass in the yellow sunlight. A big old man with white tousled hair; blown by the wind it looks like, although there is no wind. I wonder what they talk about as they walk, across the dusty grass, under the trees. Does he tell her stories? Populate the world with his adventures, exploits, friends? Fill her loneliness with his voice? And what does she tell him? That he should get a haircut? That she wants a baby but I'm too scared to let her have one?

"Who's taking me to the airport anyway?" Newcome said.

"I'm taking you," I said.

"When do we need to leave?" he said.

"Noon will be fine."

"Isn't it a three-hour drive?"

"Two hours," I said.

"What about traffic?" he said. "There might be traffic."

"Not out here," I said.

"I mean at the airport," he said.

"Not there either."

"Let's hope they have curbside check-in," he said.

"Let's hope," I said.

Newcome, my new friend.

Heavy clouds drifting into the valley when we left. A rainy morning without the rain. Catherine stood at the edge of the driveway, her toes on the gravel. "You're driving Newcome?" she said.

"Yes," I said.

"You know Billy could take him," she said.

"I'd like the drive," I said.

She was wearing loose white cotton trousers; a faded blue shirt, like a boy's. So pretty she looked. So self-contained.

"You'll be okay," I said.

"Yes," she said.

"Maybe you'll go fishing," I said.

"Maybe I will," she said.

Newcome and I zipped along the empty highway: terra-cotta hills on either side of us; boundless gray skies above. All in all it was a somber kind of day but it felt good to be out on the road, beyond the valley, away from Santa Ana. Neither of us spoke much in the car though I felt the oddest bond with Newcome, as if we were two pals cruising down this nowhere road, two guys in a car listening to the rush of the wind and the noise of the radio. For a while up in the high country we found a little station from somewhere north in Colorado that pumped out vintage rock, the classics: Eric Clapton, the Stones. Mick Jagger twanging away on *Ruby Tuesday* as we came down the pass. Cattle on a hillside. At the bottom an evil-looking, coffee-colored stream with dozens of old cars abandoned at the water's edge.

For the most part Newcome kept his head back on the seat over by the window, eyes closed as if he was resting, though I could see him beating time to the music with the palm of his hand on his knee. Then sometimes he'd open his eyes and ask, "Where are we?" like a kid. And I guess the way parents do I'd answer the real question and say, "We're not there yet." I don't know why I wanted us so badly to talk, to have a good time together, to be friends. Once or twice I remember we had a comradely discussion, about music.

"What do you like, Donald?" I think I said as we finally lost our Mick Jagger station.

"Oh, I like different things," he said, eyes open. "Do you mean old stuff or new stuff?"

"Anything," I said.

"I like a lot of the new stuff pretty much," he said. "Stray Cats. Men at Work. Did you ever hear Bananarama?"

"No, I didn't," I said.

"They're good," he said. "They're real popular in England, but the problem is they just don't get the air-play here."

"I see," I said, or something clever of that sort, but Newcome had closed his eyes again.

Years ago, of course, they didn't have the big highway. There was only the old two-lane blacktop and we mostly came down it in the rattly Land Rover with Charlie Converse at the wheel, windows wide open, dust flying, a three-hour gust of hot air in your face. But as a kid stuck out at the ranch (so it seemed), with nothing but the blessed horses, and my mother, and only sometimes my mother and father, a trip to the Albuquerque airport, even to pick up a guest and come right back, was one of the major events of the summer. My mother was the only one to pick up my father (who usually managed to come in on his own anyway), but Charlie and I drove the few others—an occasional woman friend of my mother's or Aunt Helena. "You'll only get in Charlie's way" was my mother's favorite line. "No I won't either" was mine. I never could properly explain to myself or anyone else what I found so appealing about the Albuquerque airport. "I suppose he's a boy and likes to watch the planes take off and land," I once heard my mother say, and maybe that was it.

Newcome reopened his eyes and sat up. "Of course I still like some of the old stuff," he said. "The Dead. The Stones. I guess the Stones go on forever."

"What about The Doors?" I said. It was hard imagining Newcome as a youthful Deadhead.

"Sure, I still respect The Doors," Newcome said.

"What about Santana?" I said. I just wanted him to keep talking. I wanted us to stay buddies forever.

"Yeah, Santana," Newcome said. "You like Santana?"

"I used to," I said. A white house by a river in Vermont that Tessa and I had once rented. There'd been a Santana album playing there.

"He was good," Newcome said. "I caught him once on tour. I'm telling you, the sound was excellent. I mean he sounded just like the album."

"That good?" I said.

"*Excellent*," said Newcome. "You would have really liked him that night."

"I bet I would," I said.

"Where are we now?" Newcome said, looking

around him at the ugly sandy landscape of the lowlands.

"Another forty minutes to go," I said, more or less the truth.

Once we reached the airport Newcome resumed his role of serious air traveler. First there was the curbside check-in question, answered alas by the nonexistence (at least on that day) of curbside check-in at the Albuquerque airport. Then there was the debate over which line to stand on inside.

"That one looks shorter," I said, trying to be helpful.

"But it's not 'With Tickets,' " Newcome said, having parked himself in another line, behind a Mexican family with numerous children, cartons of clothing, bags of groceries. "This one is 'With Tickets,' " he explained.

"You could probably just carry that stuff on," I said.

"I feel better checking it," Newcome said.

When he was finally checked in I suggested we get something to eat. In a way I could see that I was already losing Newcome to the traveling process, but I thought maybe with a steak and a beer we could keep on having our good time together until his flight was called. A steak and beer is what Charlie and I would have while waiting for planes. Steaks for both of us and I'd have some of his beer. "Beer's got a whole lot of nourishment anyhow," he used to say, as one who should know.

It was amazing how little the old airport had changed over the years. The same Mexican dolls. The same hanging Navaho rugs and Indian women selling jewelry. The same look about it of an old-time railroad station. Over in a far corner was a Science Fair type of exhibit on the wonders of uranium mining and right beside it, only slightly modernized, the same Fred Harvey's Lounge and Lunchroom that Converse and I used to hang out in years ago.

"You know, I used to come here as a kid," I said to Newcome, leading him inside.

"You mean you used to go to the airport to *eat*?" Newcome said.

We sat down in the lunchroom side of the room. "Let's have ourselves a good meal," I said.

"Okay," said Newcome, though I could tell that his heart wasn't in it.

I ordered a steak and a Michelob. Newcome, a grilled cheese and iced tea. "Come on, have a beer," I said.

"Okay, I'll have a beer," he said. "Actually I usually have a drink on the plane."

But even with beer and food Newcome seemed faraway, nibbling at his grilled cheese, not so much preoccupied as somewhere else, perhaps already back in LAX. But then he suddenly put down his fork and looked at me. "You know, he lives in a fucking world all his own," he said with unexpected heat.

"I guess he's not easy," I said, not really wanting to talk about my father just then.

"Not easy?" Newcome said. "Listen, we got this screenplay. It's not great. It's pretty good. But he's a great director. We might get something going with it—"

"I thought we were talking Oscars," I said.

"Let's get it made first," Newcome said. "Let's get our deal. But your father doesn't know anyone else is alive. He thinks a guy like Herb Prochnow is some kind of flunky. He thinks I'm not worth shit."

"I didn't notice he thought that," I said.

"I notice it," Newcome said. "I don't mean about the script changes. He's right about them, most of them. I mean the way he looks at you like you're not there, like you're *nothing*. The way you're talking to him and he'll pick up the phone and make a phone call. Put in a phone call, about a fucking horse! While you're still talking to him!"

"Look, I'm sorry," I said.

"*You're* sorry?" Newcome said with a laugh. "Hey, you're so cool. Nothing he does ever fazes you. I'd watch you when he'd do his numbers. The Great Director bit. Mr. Big Rancher. Mr. Know Everything. Mr. Suave with your wife. Nothing gets to you. I mean, you're confident. A fucking published author. Mr. Cool."

"The truth is I just don't get involved," I said.

"What do you mean you don't get involved?" Newcome said.

"I don't know," I said. "I don't get involved."

"Jesus, that's weird," Newcome said. "Really weird. You don't get *involved*? I guess guys like you are just different from guys like me." He glanced at his watch. "Holy Christ," he said.

"You're not late," I said.

"I haven't even made my seat selection," he said.

We paid up and marched briskly for the gate. "Look, if I overstepped I apologize," Newcome said. "I wouldn't want anyone else saying anything about my old man."

"Don't worry about it," I said.

We were standing next to the baggage-inspection counter. Newcome stuck out his hand. "When I'm your age I hope I'll have things figured out as well as you," he said with a friendly, I guess you'd have to say youthful, smile, and we shook hands, and he was gone.

With Newcome finally surrendered to air travel, I found myself (perhaps out of some strange sympathy) reluctant to leave the airport. I wandered around. Checked out the magazine stand, bought yesterday's *Los Angeles Times*. Checked out the gift shop, selling mostly off-color greeting cards and T-shirts with cute sayings. Thought maybe of having a beer at the bar. A cup of coffee. An ice-cream cone. *Mr. Suave with my wife* . . . I hadn't thought about Catherine since I left. I hadn't even thought about her when Newcome was going on about my father. Now the idea occurred to me of getting her a little something at the airport. Not a cute T-shirt or off-color greeting card. Some nice little thing. I walked over to take a look at the Indian jewelry. Bead necklaces for the airport trade. Some crudely made squash-blossom necklaces. There were some pretty turquoise earrings, but they were too expensive and maybe not pretty enough. I went to have a cup of coffee and think about the earrings. But Catherine was so vague in my mind. When I tried to picture her—her face, the way she might look with the earrings—the image blurred, or in fact never quite came together in the first place. I read the newspaper. The P.A. system announced countless flights. The so-called real world swirled all around: Japanese tourists in pointy Western boots; campers in shorts and backpacks. A man sat down beside me, an Indian I guessed, but dark, virtually black, with jet-black hair, wearing a starchy blue-denim suit. "How are you?" he said.

"I'm fine," I said, turning back to my paper.

"Look at this," he said. A high, lilting voice like someone from the Caribbean. He held up a crumpled handkerchief in his hands, then opened it to reveal a turquoise bracelet. Turquoise and silver. "Is it not beautiful?"

"Yes," I said.

"You should take it to your wife," he said.

"No, thanks," I said.

"You have a wife?"

"Yes," I said.

"Is she beautiful?"

"Yes, she's beautiful," I said.

"Well, you should buy this for her," he said. "One thousand dollars."

"No," I said.

"Nine hundred dollars."

"I'm afraid not," I said.

"What is she doing?" he said.

"What do you mean what is she doing?"

"What is she doing, your wife?"

"I don't know," I said.

"You don't know?" he said. His voice like a song. His dark, bony hands holding the blue-and-silver bracelet. "Then maybe she is not safe?"

"I don't know," I said.

"Maybe she is not safe?" he said again.

And suddenly I knew, I think in the truest, saddest way one could ever know a thing: no, she wasn't safe at all.

It felt like the longest drive I'd ever taken. Frantic and endless. Back along the same road. Not even sure what I was frantic about. They *couldn't*! went through my mind. *He* wouldn't! *She* wouldn't! But then I thought of him and realized, yes he could. He could do bloody anything to anyone! I imagined wild and unimaginable things, driving under that leaden and lowering sky, making myself nearly sick with my imaginings. And then my brain stopped. Or cleared. Or my imagination fused out for the time being. I was doing over ninety on the speedometer and thought, This is crazy, this is being truly crazy. What am I worried about? My father and my wife? My old father, my new wife. I'll come back and there they'll be, he in his study yelling at Herb Prochnow on the phone, she wandering back from the creek with her fly rod. That's what I'll find. But in the crannies of my mind I still saw specters, awful shapes, a blurry nightmare of possibilities. And I didn't let the needle drop much below seventy-five.

It must have been around six o'clock when I got back. A gray light everywhere, covering the valley. The old house white and still. No wind blowing in the trees. No rain as yet. You could see the horses down in the pasture, their tails swishing in familiar rhythms. I went inside. Not a sound anywhere. The downstairs rooms suffused with the same gray pallor as the outside; an absence of light I guess you'd call it, though at the time it seemed like an absence of life. Then I heard the splash of water running in the kitchen. He's out there making coffee, I thought gladly. Catherine's fixing something. Maria's rinsing vegetables. You can't imagine how reassuring it was to hear one of those everyday household noises. I almost ran to the kitchen door and pushed it open. Trent was standing in front of the sink, his back to me, washing something off his hands.

"Trent?" I said, one of those foolish stage questions. He was wearing only an undershirt above his trousers and I noticed there were freckles all over his shoulders and arms. "Where's everybody?"

"I just got back," he said a little primly. I had the feeling I had embarrassed him in his undershirt. He started to dry his hands on a paper towel. "I haven't seen anybody."

"You don't know where Catherine is?" I said.

"I haven't seen anybody," he said.

"Or my father?" I said. "Or Maria?"

He shook his head. "The truck is gone," he said. "They must have gone somewhere in the truck. I don't think Maria came up today."

"Thanks very much, Trent," I said, trying to manage some degree of composure.

"Don't mention it," he said, starting to put on his shirt, which had been hanging on one of the kitchen chairs.

I went upstairs, down the long quiet corridor. She'll be there in our room, I thought. Asleep. The door was closed. I knocked softly first, then a bit harder. Opened the door. The room was empty and in a strange kind of disarray. The bedcover half on the floor. A pillow on the floor. The chair from my worktable lying on its side. Catherine's sneakers in the doorway to the bathroom. I ran downstairs again.

"You've got to tell me where they are," I said to Trent.

"I don't know where they are," he said.

The gray light everywhere outside, a deeper gray, like dusk on an autumn day. Gray fields. Gray willows near the creek. What I first saw was her red headband through the willows. A speck of red. A plume of red. Not moving. She was sitting at the edge of the stream, perhaps fifty yards away, knees up, arms around her legs. "Catherine!" I called. It was all so quiet save for the rippling of the stream, and for my shoes treading across the ground. "Catherine!" I called again, but then without a word or glance she got to her feet and moved through the willows out of sight.

Out in the field. Her back to me in the middle of the field. Her white blouse against the gray sky. The barn behind her in the distance. "Catherine!" I said. She turned around then and I don't know what it was I saw on her face, or in those eyes, that made my heart freeze—in mid-greeting—but freeze it did. "What do you want?" she said. There was no recognizable temperature to that voice. Not fear, not hurt, not anger. Her eyes were set deep in her face. Her arms hung at her sides. The top part of her blouse was torn.

"What happened?" I said.

"Nothing happened," she said, just looking at me, the top of her blouse hanging loosely like a torn flap; her breathing audible as if she'd been running.

"I don't believe you," I said.

"What do you think happened?" she said.

"I don't know," I said.

"Your father made a pass at me," she said, and there was a tiny crease, a curl, beside her mouth which made it almost look as if she was smiling.

"He did *what*?" I said, taking her by both arms.

"You heard me," she said. She seemed so calm, and with that little smile around her mouth. I was shaking her by the arms. "Stop it, you're hurting me," she said, breaking away from me.

"What *happened*?" I said.

"I don't want to talk about it," she said, starting back off across the field.

She walked and I walked with her. She started to run and I ran beside her. Past willows, willow branches. Again beside the creek. The splash of water. Stones. We crossed the creek. A crazy game being played by children who are no longer children. "Stop, Catherine!" I called. And, "Please, stop!" I didn't want to hurt her. But then I took her by the arm again, and whether she fell or what I don't know except we were both on the ground. She kicked her feet. I lay across her legs. "Stay still," I said. She wriggled out but then stayed where she was, a few feet away, on her knees, her face white and shining in the twilight. "What do you want to know?" she said.

"I want to know what happened," I said.

"He tried to kiss me," she said.

"Where?" I said.

"What do you mean where?"

"Where did it happen?" I said. "Where were you?"

"In what *room*?" she said.

"Yes," I said.

"Downstairs," she said. "I was downstairs in the living room. On the couch. Looking at a photo album."

"And then?" I said.

"Why are you asking me all these questions?" she said. "He came in and sat down beside me. He was sitting beside me and we were both looking at the photo album . . ."

"And?"

"I don't know," she said.

"You do know," I said.

"He was sitting there beside me," she said, "and then he put his hand on my face."

"His hand?"

"On the side of my face," she said. "Then he kissed me."

"So he did kiss you?"

"Yes."

"You said he tried to kiss you."

"It felt like the same thing," she said.

Infinite silence. The light fading. Catherine sitting there a few feet from me in her torn blouse.

"What kind of kiss?" I said.

"What do you mean what kind of kiss?" she said.

"You know what I mean."

"I don't remember," she said.

"Just a kiss?"

"I don't know."

"A real kiss?"

"Yes," she said. "I guess so."

"My *father*?" I said.

"I don't want to talk about it anymore," she said.

The rippling of the stream nearby. A wind came up; the evening wind from down the canyon. She was sitting sideways to me, her arms around her knees again. "He wasn't supposed to do it," she said. "Don't you see, he wasn't supposed to do it . . ."

She was walking slowly back up the road.

"What else happened?" I said.

"Nothing," she said.

"I don't believe you," I said. "You were together on the couch . . ."

"I went upstairs. As soon as I could I went upstairs."

"Why upstairs?" I said.

She stopped in the road. We were face to face. "Because I was scared. What do you think?" she said. "I went up and lay down on the bed. I wanted to hide, to pull the covers over my head."

"And then?" I said.

"And then he came in."

"He came in the room?"

"He sat down on the side of the bed," she said. "He said he was sorry he scared me. He was being really nice, like a father again. And then he started to stroke me."

"Stroke you where?" I said.

"First my arm, and then up here," she said, indicating near her breast. "And then my leg."

"He was stroking your leg?" I said.

"Yes."

"All the way up your leg?"

"I don't remember," she said. "I didn't know what to do." I was holding her by the arms, shaking her. "Let me go!" she said.

"All the way up?"

"Yes," she said. "No."

"My own fucking father!" I said. "That's a joke, isn't it?"

"I swear he never touched me."

"My own father trying to fuck you," I said.

"Don't say that!"

"My own father trying to fuck you!"

"No! No! No!" she said. "It wasn't like that!"

"Miss Innocence," I said.

"No!" she said.

"The shy little ranch princess."

"Goddamn it, you *left* me there with him!" she said.

"And were you waiting down in the willows for him to finish the job?"

And then she slapped me, hard and stinging. "Oh, I wish I had," she said.

It was dark when I drove down the road to find him, though find him where I wasn't sure. I don't think I'd ever been so angry in my life. I felt about to burst with anger—mad rage. All those years of his not caring, not helping, not loving! Jesus, not loving! Loving no one but himself! The almighty father! And now for him to try to take the one precious thing I had—and to take it so carelessly, heedlessly, like a spoiled medieval baron! No, I vowed in the darkness not to lose my anger this time, not to let it dissipate, trail off into stoic adolescent sulks, but to keep it whole inside me, hot and violent. Such a black night it had become too; pitch-black as they say. Not a star in the sky. I drove down the road without a destination, other than to find him and have it out; to have that confrontation I'd been putting off all my life. And then ahead of me in the glare of headlights I saw something—not him; a mailbox: the white mailbox with a miniature horse atop it that marked the turnoff to the Bonaventura place. And knew instantly where he was.

. . .

Their road wasn't hard to follow, though it was longer and bumpier than I expected. A line of buck fence on the left. Fields on the right. Dust from the dirt road in the headlight beams. Far off in one of the fields there was a metal barn—a lonesome ugly thing—illuminated by one of those all-night lamps. That one bright ghostly yellow light in all that emptiness. A little bridge. A stretch of gravel. Then up a hill and down a hill—partway down it. The Bonaventura house was there at the bottom, sheltered by trees; its long low roof and adobe walls looking dangerous and secret, like a fortress.

I parked the car above the house and walked down the rest of the way. Below me was a circular driveway paved with flagstones, a little tree or something in the center of it, larger trees on the perimeter. Believe me, the night was dark, and with my headlights off it was hard to see the proverbial hand before one's face. Bushes, trees, everything was black. Even the house itself was dark, at least the front of it, except for a tiny light in the ground just near the door, and then a brighter glow coming from the back, where the bedroom was.

I walked down the driveway, feeling like a burglar, feeling crazy. But then I saw it: the truck; his truck. The pickup parked on the far side of the driveway, almost hidden under one of the trees. I was making my way across the flagstones when my foot struck a piece of wood. I reached down to pick it up and as I did a light in the front of the house came on and the door opened. "Who's out there?" Priscilla Bonaventura called.

I kept walking toward the house.

"Who's there?" she said. "Who is that?"

She was standing in the doorway in a long robe, one hand holding the door, the other a small revolver. "Tom, is that you?" she called.

I walked right by her, the piece of wood clutched in my hand.

"Tom!" she called, this time behind me.

The inside of the house was hard to see in the faint light. A conventional living room on the left; a kitchen on the right. A small lamp was lit in the hallway, but most of the light in the house was coming from the back. I went quickly down the corridor. Not far to go; a short corridor. A half-open doorway. The corner of a bed. I pushed the door open but the room was empty. A television set was turned on near the bed, with the sound off.

"Where is he?" I said to Priscilla, who was standing behind me, still holding the revolver in her hand but pointed at the floor.

"Tom, what are you doing here?" she said. "I could have shot you." She put the revolver away in a little cabinet near the bed and turned off the television set.

"Where is he?" I said.

"Where is who?"

"Where's my father?"

"He's not here," she said. "Why should he be here?"

"Goddamit, I know he's here."

"Please put that stick down," she said.

"Never mind the stick."

I threw open the bathroom door.

"Your father's not here," she said.

"Why is his truck here then?"

"I don't think it is," she said.

"That's your truck?"

"Of course it's our truck."

"I don't believe you," I said.

"Why don't you check?" she said. "Would you like to see the registration papers?"

I slammed the piece of wood against the bed in frustration.

"Why should your father be here anyway?" Priscilla said.

"That's my business," I said.

"*Your* business!" she said. "You come barging in here in the dark, brandishing that stick and scaring me half to death, and then you say it's *your* business!"

"Stop talking about the damn stick," I said, dropping it on the bed.

"Do you want a drink?" she said.

"No," I said.

"Well, I do," she said.

We left the bedroom and went back into the living room. She poured herself a drink from a bottle of bourbon and sat down on the gold-covered couch near the fireplace. I was—I don't know—standing, sitting, pacing, everywhere and nowhere.

"Tom, what's all this about?" she said. She was balancing her glass on the arm of the couch—one of those little blue Mexican glasses.

"It's between him and me," I said.

"Him and you?" she said. "Father and son. God, men are so relentless and exhausting—"

"I don't think it's all that funny," I said.

"My, you *are* worked up, aren't you?" she said. "Well, I don't think it's that funny either. For years and years I used to watch my brother and father. In fact, it's about all I can remember of either of them—Lewis and Daddy: two rocks grinding away at one another, just grinding away. The sad thing is they really loved each other too."

"I sure as hell don't love my father," I said.

"Maybe not," she said. "Come and sit down."

"No," I said.

She shrugged and looked away. "I ought to go and do something to my face," she said.

"Go ahead," I said.

"Don't you know you're supposed to say 'Don't bother'?" she said, getting up and going down the hall.

I thought I'd leave then but I didn't. Priscilla came back in a few minutes with what I guess is called some color on her face and with her hair brushed out.

"Please sit down, Tom," she said.

I sat down.

"Supposing I'd been here with George?" she said.

"George is away in Colorado or somewhere," I said.

"True," she said. She took a sip from her drink and handed the glass to me. I took a swallow and gave it back. "What are you looking at?" she said.

I didn't say anything.

She reached over and placed a hand on my arm. "Thomas Avery," she said.

"Don't do that," I said.

"Don't do what?" she said.

She was smiling at me in a funny way, like a girl I guess, but not like any girl I could remember. The green gown was hanging loosely from her shoulders so you could see the outline of her breasts. I moved my arm from under her hand and touched her hair.

"I get tired of long hair," she said.

Her hair felt soft like feathers.

"When I was a girl, that's the one nice thing people would say about me. 'Priscilla's got such lovely hair . . .' "

Her hair felt like flowers, like ferns.

" 'Priscilla's crowning glory,' Daddy used to say," she said. "Isn't that a quaint expression?"

"You're talking too much," I said.

Priscilla was looking at me. I had stopped stroking her hair. I'm not sure what thought or feeling was in her eyes; maybe nothing. But then I kissed her. A clumsy kiss really. I could feel her mouth tighten beneath mine. I could feel her pulling back, but then she said, "Don't, Tom," and there was something in the way she said it that made me kiss her again, and then her lips opened. And then what else did she say: "You mustn't." And: "Not here."

I remember I said, "Here."

She was kneeling in front of me on the couch, her hair askew; the green gown had slipped off one of her shoulders so that most of one breast was exposed.

"No," she said.

But then the green gown was on the floor, along

with my trousers and shoes, and she was lying under me on the couch, her breasts against my shirt, and I was inside her. "You're going to hurt me," she said. "No I'm not," I said. I rode her hard. Soft breasts bouncing. Many cries. At times her eyes would roll far up under her eyelids. Hands clutching me to her. Her body, I remember, was ampler than I thought. Not such a skinny lady after all; not such a lady.

Afterward I could feel her fingers tracing patterns on the back of my shirt. Then they stopped. "You bastard," she said.

While I stumbled around putting back on the few clothes I'd taken off, Priscilla sat in a corner of the couch, first holding the gown against her nakedness, then pulled it on again, tugging it down below her knees.

"*Why*?" she said. "Why me?"

"I don't know," I said.

She got slowly to her feet. "I never did this with anyone but George since we were married," she said. And, "Do you want that drink?"

"No, thanks," I said.

She had her back to me at the far end of the room, standing before a mirror. "So, I guess you'll be going now?" she said.

"I guess I will," I said.

She turned around. An older woman holding a hairbrush in her hand. Her face tired as if from traveling. "Well then, goddamit go!" she said. "Goddamit *go*!"

Old enough to be my mother, the thought went through my head. Perhaps not exactly true in terms of strict chronology. But not untrue either. True enough. Else why did I think it, why did the thought keep running through my head? Oh, Jesus, what a thought! And let me tell you, the strangest thing was that it was a thought without shame attached to it; a kind of deep internal geologic upset, but no shame. With each passing moment, first sitting in my car outside her house, then beginning the drive back to the ranch, I kept expecting shame to find me, kept reaching out for shame to reassure me, like a policeman, with its presence. But I knew it wouldn't; that it wasn't there. What was there instead was a memory or dream of long hair and soft skin and pendant breasts. But whose long hair was it in the end? Whose soft skin and pendant breasts? I was driving through the thick darkness and came near the end of the Bonaventura road, where it connected to the valley road, to ours. And stopped the car. My mind a daze. My mind a maze. Priscilla on the couch, the gold-covered couch! But then, as if some circuit shut down inside my brain, I couldn't see Priscilla's face anymore. The more I tried I couldn't see her face. Then couldn't see the gold-covered couch. The long green gown. Only my mother smiling at me. Yes, unmistakably *her* face! But not my old mother, before she died. My young, my younger mother, with her girlish smile, her dancing eyes, and yes that long hair. I laid my head back on the car seat, in a kind of surrender so it felt. My mother come to claim me. My beautiful, beguiling, lonely mother. My mother coming down the stairs somewhere in one of her dresses. My mother standing by the mantelpiece shaking her hair. "Be a dear and light me a cigarette, Tommy." Her soft thin arm and slender fingers. "Be a dear and make me a drink, Tommy." My mother standing in her bedroom getting dressed. Half dressed. "Come and talk to me, Tommy. Stay awhile, Tommy. Talk to me, Tommy . . ." Her slip and stockings. Pink and silky. The pale skin above the stocking tops. The shape of her breasts. The warmth of her breasts. "Oh, damn these zippers. I'm all thumbs tonight. You've got small hands, don't you, Tommy? Clever hands. Sensitive hands . . ." The milky color of her skin beneath the dress. The smoothness of her skin below the lace. "Oh, thank you, Tommy. You're such a help. Such a good boy . . ." Her lips red with lipstick. Her scent filling the room, floating in the air. A perfume smelling of lilacs. The fragrance of lilacs everywhere. Her smell. Even the ranch smelled of lilacs when she was there. You could breathe it on the stairs or in the hallway after she'd passed through. The sweet smell of lilacs . . . I opened my eyes. Got out of the car. Oh God, I missed her so! And could feel her somewhere out in the night air, out in the darkness. Remembering her hand on my head. In my hair. The way she used to stroke my hair as a kid. Even just before she died, she stroked my hair. "My good boy, Tommy. My good son. You never let me down, did you, Tommy . . ." I could feel the tears streaming down my face. Helpless tears. Tears like a wail, like a lament. Tears like love. Tears like mourning, far worse than mourning. Oh, it's frightening to *feel*—to feel such loss! I was on my knees in the darkness, in a field I couldn't see, blubbering like a kid. I'm not proud of the moment, please believe me. But there it was. There I was. Lost like one of God's children in a pagan night. A boy lost in a world of dangerous men, crying for his mama. The moon goddess. And there above me, far off to the right, above the mountains, was a new hazy glow behind the black, blowing clouds. Not a goddess but the moon itself. And far down the road ahead of me, coming from the ranch, were two headlights, moving in silence so it seemed, and fast; a car's headlights, not a truck's, coming down the road, then past me standing in the field, then vanished. I looked up into the sky again and saw for the first time two stars, a sliver of the moon, for the sky was clearing. I thought of Catherine at the ranch and went back to the car. And remembered Priscilla too; that crazy moment. Could see

Priscilla Bonaventura clearly, with her own face. Not my mother but the woman I'd just fucked. Fucked on her gold-covered couch. And as I started up the car it struck me, with what's called the simplicity of truth, that my loss was probably in the end just this. I wasn't such a good boy after all. I wasn't such a boy. No, not at all.

The ranch was buried in darkness, not a light on anywhere. A wash of moonlight on the trees and roof. No sign of the old man's truck. I opened the front door quietly and right away knocked into something with my foot. One suitcase, two suitcases. Catherine's suitcases. Without turning on the light I climbed the stairs, went down the corridor. The door to our room was open. Moonlight spilling over an empty room. But tidied up this time; no sheets or pillows on the floor, no sneakers in the doorway. Rarely have I felt a room to be so empty. I sat down for a moment on the bed, now smooth and flat, a place no one had lately slept in (or had much fun in either), running the palm of my hand over the cover as if somehow that dumb rhythmic gesture might bring Catherine back.

On my way downstairs the thought occurred to me that my father might be hiding somewhere in the house; it was a night for crazy thoughts so why not that one? But I could always tell when he was around, when he was home, and I knew he wasn't. Perhaps I should wake up Trent, but what could or would Trent do about anything? My wife's left me, Trent. My father's won. Could Trent fix that? I went into the living room, that big silent room, walked over to the windows through which you could see the barest outline of the barn and corrals and the dark shapes of trees. I don't know what I was looking for. I suppose I was waiting for my father to come back. And then what? Would I find another stick somewhere and strike him with it? Would David finally slay Goliath? Somewhere behind me I heard a sound, the barest of sounds. I turned around, saw nothing but an empty room in moonlight. Then over on the couch, something . . . someone moving . . . Catherine: trying to sit up, rubbing her eyes.

"Tom?" she said.

"What are you doing here?" I said. My voice harsh with strain, though I was so glad to see her I could hardly speak.

"I'm not doing anything," she said. "Trying to wake up." She sat up, facing me on the couch. "I was so scared you'd left. Where did you go?"

"It's a long story," I said. "Looking for my father."

"I'm so glad you're here," she said.

I held her and kissed her, kissed her cheeks, her lips, her mouth.

"I love you," she said. And, "I'm so sleepy I can't wake up."

"Don't wake up," I said.

"There was a car," she said.

"What car?"

"I don't know," she said. "I think it was the car

that Maria comes in sometimes. It just drove around and then went off. Don't go away again."

"I saw your suitcases," I said.

"What do you mean?" she said. I was on the couch, holding her in my arms.

"Your suitcases in the hallway," I said. "Were you going away?"

"Without you?" she said.

"I didn't know," I said.

"I thought *you* wanted to go," she said. "I just wanted to go with you." She settled down deeper in my arms, her head on my lap. "God, you're all so crazy sometimes," she said.

"Are you cold?" I said, thinking I could bring her a blanket or better still take her up to bed.

"No, I'm not cold," she said. "Don't move. Just hold me. Say you're back."

"I'm back," I said.

I could feel her sleeping in my arms, could hear her breathing. Then I must have fallen asleep myself, I don't know for how long. The telephone woke me, like an alarm. Ringing in the darkness. My father's office, bedroom, kitchen. Rang twice. Three times. Then someone picked it up.

"Who was that?" Catherine said.

"I don't know," I said.

"I mean who picked it up?"

"I guess Trent," I said.

"You mean Trent's here?" she said, sitting up.

I heard the sound of a door opening down the corridor and got up to see. Trent was standing outside the guest room, tucking a shirt into his trousers.

"I need your car," he said.

"Who was that?"

"Never mind," he said. "I need your car."

"Was that my father?" I said.

We were both standing in the hallway; Catherine's suitcases on the floor. "No, it wasn't," he said. Trent's face looked old and creased, and there was something on his lips that glistened like lipstick.

"The hell it wasn't," I said.

"I said it wasn't him," he said. "But I need those car keys."

Catherine was standing beside me. "What's happened?" she said.

"Nothing yet," Trent said. "Give me the car keys, Tom." He stuck out his hand.

"No," I said. He didn't say anything; he just stood there with his hand out in front of him, looking at me. Then I said, "Trent, tell me where he is."

"Tom, I don't think—" he began.

"Just tell me where he is," I said.

"He's at the Cortez," he said, lowering his hand. "Do you know where that is?"

"Yes," I said.

"I'll come with you," Catherine said.

"No, I don't think so."

"Please," she said.

"You'll be safe here this time," I said, walking toward the door. "Trent, what was the message on the phone?"

"That Sánchez was looking for him," he said.

I suppose I should have thought about Sánchez but I didn't. Or about Catherine but I didn't. Even about Priscilla but I didn't. What I was thinking about was *him.* Not the first time in my life that my emotions, focus, supposed rationality, whatever, had been diverted in his direction, no matter what public-relations announcements I might have made to the contrary: *I never think about my old man! We never talk! I have nothing to do with him!* And so on. In fact, it's struck me more than once that one of the great unfairnesses of life is that the parent who does the least for you is usually the one you think about most. That is, the parent who most attends you, worries about you, notices you and bores you most by noticing (Wear your overshoes! Do your homework! Come home by midnight!) is frequently the one who sets you on the path to freedom—at least such slight freedom as is ever achieved in these matters. But the cool parent, the absent parent, the cat-burglar parent, the demon-lover parent, the glamorous ghost parent is the one who haunts you for the rest of your life. The highwayman's face seen through the stagecoach window! The man with the blue silk scarf glimpsed in the hotel bar in Rome! I've tried to remember what was in my mind as I drove down the road for the last time that night, and I think it was something like this: that he was waiting for me somewhere at the end of that road; that if I got there—wherever *there* was—I'd finally find him, have him; that he'd be *still* at last, ready to listen. And it was only crossing the bridge into the old town (with the abandoned cattle truck still sitting there, tilted on its limp tires) that another thought occurred to me: that he might already be dead.

The little town was shut up for the night. Closed down like a dead place. A couple of the stores boarded up as if not expected to reopen. A single streetlight at the corner near the old Texaco station. Two scrawny spotted dogs prowling the main street. A red neon sign flashing on and off . . . on and off . . . in the window of the Farmacia-Drugs. No pile of boxes lying out front, but this time a pyramid of gravel at the entrance to the general store. The Cortez was about two miles out of town, due west along the old county road. A notorious roadhouse in its day. Honest-to-God hookers and gambling (even "out-of-state gamblers" according to report) and celebrated brawls—this being in that glorious time after the war when people, even in such places as Santa Ana, dreamed of finding uranium in their back yards. I think it was built originally as a travelers' hotel by a German couple named Gunther. (Mrs. Gunther, so the story went, had been some kind of relative of D. H. Lawrence's wife.) "I'm tellin' you, they had it painted white like a convent," Charlie Converse told me with some amazement, "and they sure ran a *clean* place. Too bad nobody wanted krauts around during the war." Most of the white paint and much of the cleanliness was gone by the time I first saw it. A string of colored light bulbs ran around the roof. Drunken cowboys three-deep at the bar. Waitresses in little short skirts. Mysterious rooms in back where really serious (presumably out-of-state) gambling went on. "Kid, don't ever let me catch you bettin' money here till you're seventeen years old," said Charlie Converse, an unlikely father figure the more I think about him, who'd sometimes let me wait near the bar while he picked up a six-pack, my head reeling from the smell of smoke and beer and waitresses and God knows what else.

But now at night, from a few hundred yards down the road, the Cortez seemed small and drab. A flaky pastel paint job on the outside. No colored light bulbs on the roof, but the remains of an orange neon sign with two or three of the letters missing. An Airstream trailer was parked in back where the parking lot used to be. A mattress and box spring with most of the springs sticking out lay on the ground. A line of wash stretched from a corner of the Cortez to a little shack nearby. There were a couple of pickups parked haphazardly on the grass, also a phone-company truck, also a car without any wheels. My father's truck was sitting right across the street next to a phone pole.

I was walking over to check it out when a dog suddenly started to bark loudly and pulled on its chain. Just then the screen door in the front of the Cortez opened and a man stuck his head out, at first I thought because he owned the dog, which was large and vicious, and was going to tell it to stop, but he had no eyes for the dog, only for me. He stood there at the top of the steps just staring at me, then finally went down two steps, nimbly, quickly, and said, "Come inside!" and then, "In here, please!"—more a command than an invitation, gesturing impatiently with one hand.

I followed him in through the screen door. It was the same big room I remembered as a kid, but dour and quiet. Dark. I guess there were some little tables, chrome and plastic, which were new; a pool table where a large, soft-bellied Indian in a tractor cap was playing by himself. The only other people in the room were four or five men at the bar, none of whom turned around. A video game was standing where the jukebox used to be.

I peered around the gloomy interior for my father, relieved at first he wasn't there.

The man who'd summoned me inside—olive-skinned with wavy black hair and steel-rimmed spectacles—had gone behind the bar.

"I'm looking for my father, Samuel Avery," I said.

None of the men at the bar said anything. The man behind the bar seemed to be expecting me to say more.

"Is he here?" I said.

From time to time he glanced away from me to the screen door as if he thought someone was about to come through it, but no one did. "Sam Avery your father?" he said. "Mr. Avery?"

"Yes," I said.

"Upstairs," he said.

"Upstairs?" I said. I remembered another thing Converse said to me: "No going upstairs till you're seventeen either."

Then he reached across the bar and took hold of my arm, a tight grip too. "Go quick," he said in the way people finally say what they mean.

At the far end of the room there was a narrow flight of stairs, steep and rickety. Then a long corridor, also narrow; peeling green paint on the walls. A single light bulb overhead. A row of doors half open along each side. Little rooms, dark and empty. Linoleum underfoot. The smell of something stale in the air, like sweat or urine. The last door on the corridor was closed; no, not quite closed, and through the opening you could see a sliver of light.

I pushed it open. The room was in shadows, the light (such as it was) coming from a bathroom in the rear. A tiny room like all the others. One bed against the wall; a metal bed I think. Maria was sitting up in the bed; maybe not quite sitting up. My father, naked, on his stomach, was lying sprawled across her. Around his waist and legs a tangle of sheets. The bed a mess of rumpled sheets. His naked white back. Maria's brown arms around him, bare brown breasts, black hair, red splotches on the sheets next to her. I remember thinking, Maria's bleeding. My father stretched across her, his head on her belly, his hair white and matted, his eyes closed as if he were sleeping. Maria clutching him in her brown arms. Maria bleeding. The flesh on his shoulders seemed so old. Naked. Then I saw the red beneath his arms, the red stains coming from his chest and ribs, *his* stains, *him* bleeding . . . "Oh, Jesus" is the only thing I knew to say. Maria looking neither at him nor at me. Just holding him.

Maria shook her head. Just that: a shake of the head, side to side. No, it seemed to say. Or, stay away.

"Maria, what happened?" I said again. I was right up close, kneeling beside the bed. I could see the blood all over her hands and running down his side.

"No touch," she said.

I put a hand on his back anyway.

"He dead," Maria said.

His skin was warm. In fact, I could feel him breathing. "He's not dead," I said.

"He dead," Maria said. "Sánchez shoot."

"Maria, we've got to get him out of here," I said, standing up. I put a hand on her shoulder, I suppose to urge her out of bed, but then realized she was naked.

"What are you doing?" she said.

"We have to get him to a doctor," I said.

Just then my father stirred, opened one eye, then both eyes. "Who the hell is that?" he said in a raspy, whispery voice, squinting right at me.

"Maria, get up and put some clothes on," I said.

"Tom?" he said.

"Dad, can you move?"

"Of course I can move," he said in that whispery voice. He turned on his side, grunting a little, and tried sitting up. "Goddamn, that stings," he said.

"I bet it stings," I said. "Do you think you can stand up?"

"Not without my pants," he said. "Get me my pants."

A fine time for modesty, I thought, but rummaged anyway beneath the bed, among the bedsheets, for trousers and shirt and underwear and whatever. "Look, just put the trousers on," I said, watching him struggle with his undershorts.

"I don't need to be told how to get dressed," he said.

I rummaged around some more, found Maria's dress and handed it to her. My father was more or less sitting on the edge of the bed, pulling his clothes on an inch at a time, wincing whenever he moved his left shoulder, where most of the drying blood had collected. "Do you want me to wash that off for you?" I said.

"Water in this place could kill you," he said. "Maria, where's the bottle?"

"No more drink, Sam," she said.

"Give me the goddamn bottle, Maria," he said. Maria fished under her side of the bed and handed him a pint of what looked like bourbon, which he took with one hand and poured over his shoulder, yelling,

"Jesus Christ, that stings! Jesus Christ, that stings!" as the whiskey ran into and over the wound and splashed on the sheets.

I took a pillowcase off one of the pillows, tore it apart, and started to wrap the strips around his shoulder in a makeshift bandage.

"What the hell is that?" he said, trying to pull it off.

"Will you for Christ sakes be still," I said.

"What in hell is it?" he said.

"It's a goddamn bandage," I said. "Ever hear of one?"

"Don't make it too tight," he said.

Finally he got to his feet, not real sturdy you might say, but not too bad either for an old man with a bullet in his shoulder. "Put your weight on me," I said.

"What for?" he said.

"Just do as I say," I said.

We made our way slowly down the narrow corridor. "Maria, you there?" my father said.

"Sure I'm here," Maria said behind us.

"This place is a shithole," he said.

"Now you say shithole," Maria said. "I always say shithole."

As we started down the stairs I could feel him begin to fall. "No you don't," I said, though there wasn't much room for me to grab on to him and hold him upright.

"I think I may just slip a little," he said, suddenly very sleepy.

"No, goddamit you won't," I said.

"I may," he said.

"No you *won't*," I said, and bit by bit we got him down the stairs.

"Those were some stairs," he said when we reached the bottom.

The big gloomy room was exactly as I'd left it. The Indian in the tractor cap was still playing pool. The five men were still at the bar. The bartender or owner or whoever the man with the spectacles was walked over to us. "Mr. Avery, I'm very sorry," he said.

"Go fuck yourself, Henry," my father said.

"I don't want trouble," the man said.

I steered my father across to the screen door, his arm around my neck and shoulders. Just before we got outside I turned to Maria and in an undertone asked her, "Where's Sánchez now?"

"Who cares about Sánchez?" she said loudly. "He is a little man. Little—do you know? Very small. I kill him if I see him."

I put my father in the front seat and Maria in back.

"What kind of car is this?" he said, once again very drowsy.

"A Volvo," I said. To Maria I said, "Where's the nearest hospital?"

"No hospital here," she said.

"Where's the nearest doctor?" I said.

"No doctor," she said.

"Oh, Christ," I said. My father's eyes were closed and his breathing seemed very faint.

But then he woke up again briefly. "Doc Loomis," he said. "Go right on Fourth Street. Ten miles down the road. Can't miss it." He looked over at me, then reached for my hand. “Tom,” he said, with a truly odd kind of smile. “Fancy seeing you here, Tom.” I held his hand and returned it to his lap, but by then he was asleep again and I was looking for the turn at Fourth Street.

We reached Doc Loomis's place along with the first dim light of dawn. A two-story white house out in the middle of nowhere, with a picket fence around it and a mailbox that said R. E. Loomis and a kid's swing and a horse trailer parked in back next to an aluminum shed. The sky overhead looked empty and enormous but there was the beginning of a pink glow over in the east, really a beautiful rosy hue, everything flat and still and peaceful as a little pond, and my father unconscious in the front seat of the car.

I kept banging on the front door until at last it opened. A young man standing there, maybe thirty years old and maybe not, short fair hair and pale blue pajamas. I figured him to be Doc Loomis's son but just to be safe I said, "Doc Loomis?"

"Yes," he said. Clean-cut and wary as a second lieutenant.

"I've got a patient for you," I said. "I think he needs help pretty bad."

He walked with me to the car, growing younger

and shorter with every step. "Holy smokes, it's Mr. Avery," he said when he drew close. "Do you know what's the matter with him?"

"He's got a bullet somewhere near his shoulder," I said.

"Oh boy," said Doc Loomis gravely.

Just then Maria climbed out the back of the car and went around to the front and opened the door next to my father. "Get out, Sam," she said, tugging him by the sleeve of his hurt arm.

"He said we should bring him here," I said.

"He did?" Doc Loomis said.

"Aren't you a doctor?" I said.

"I'm a vet," he said.

My father woke up with a start. "Goddamn, watch what you're doing," he said to Maria. Then he saw Doc Loomis. "Hey, Doc," he said. "You got to fix me up."

"Gee, I don't know, Mr. Avery," Doc Loomis said.

"Sure you can," my father said, trying to get out of the car but falling back on the seat.

"You better bring him in," I heard Doc Loomis say. I half lifted the old man up, half propped him up, and with Maria trotting along at his other side we hauled him into the house, following Doc Loomis down a corridor, through a kitchen, and then another door into what must have been the inside of the shed: a large room with a concrete floor, and a metal sink, and rows of jars and bottles, and a kind of leather harness hanging from the ceiling, and a huge square stainless-steel table, and with the creamy white walls all covered with photographs of dogs and horses.

But now Loomis had put on a green doctor's coat over his pajamas, and my father's shirt was off as well as the makeshift bandage, and Loomis was swabbing cotton around the bloody place on my father's shoulder. A young woman appeared in jeans and T-shirt, stringy blond hair and upturned nose—Mrs. Loomis I guessed. My father lay strangely passive on one side of the big metal table while Mrs. Loomis brought in and set up a folding table in the back of the room.

"Looks like he's lost some blood," Doc Loomis said.

"Can you do it?" I said.

"I sure can try," he said.

Loomis and I carried the old man over to the smaller table, a massage or exercise table it looked like, covered by a white sheet.

"How about some coffee?" Mrs. Loomis asked.

"No, thanks," I said.

Loomis gave him a shot up in his arm, just below the shoulder. Then he cleaned off the wound some more. Then he started poking around inside with a nasty-looking metal thing. Actually, I didn't mind the poking around—the bloody part—too much. But what was hard to take was the way my father looked. So white in the face. So old and helpless. His mouth I remember was open like an old bird's beak. I noticed that Maria was no longer in the room, so I stepped out of the shed, back into the house, to see if she was there. I found her in the living room, on her knees, surrounded by early-American-type furniture and flowered chintz cushions, tears rolling down her cheeks, praying.

I phoned the ranch, got Trent, and told him what had happened. At first he didn't say anything. Just silence for a while so that I thought maybe the line was dead. "Do you want me to call the papers?" he finally said.

"He's not dead," I said.

"No, of course," he said. I asked him for Catherine but he said she was asleep. "Well, wake her up and tell her," I said. "Wake her and tell her."

I went back in the shed and watched the Loomises work on my father. Doc Loomis all business in his green doctor's coat and blue pajama trousers and bedroom slippers. Blood all over one side of the sheet.

Maria was standing beside me, silent, her eyes dry. I thought of her kneeling amid the flowery chintz. "Please God make him all right, make him all right," I said under my breath, far under my breath, in the silence of my mind, the first prayer I'd uttered in I don't know how many years.

"There's the bugger," I heard Doc Loomis say.

For some reason I was watching Maria but her expression didn't change.

"Don't we have anything smaller than a number 12?" Doc Loomis said.

"Don't you remember, we used up all the 10 on Bernard's collie," Mrs. Loomis said.

When they were done my father lay on his back, asleep, bandages all over the left side of his chest and shoulder. His face was still white as a ghost. White stubble on his cheeks and chin. A smell of whiskey near his mouth. His other arm—his good arm—lay draped across his stomach. I reached down to touch it, to touch his arm, to touch something of him; but he looked so frail, so breakable, that I couldn't.

"How about some coffee now?" said Mrs. Loomis. Already a few lines around her young eyes; a country girl who'd grown up fast. She pulled a clean sheet up over my father's chest.

We had coffee in the Loomises' kitchen, in their kitchen alcove. Doc Loomis, his wife, and now two young children, a girl and boy who glided in and out in undershorts, eating doughnuts. Maria had stayed behind in the shed with my father. I thanked the Loomises or tried to; wanted to thank Doc Loomis sincerely and profusely, but he seemed not to want to talk about it anymore. What he wanted to talk about was horses, my father's horses, some shots they were supposed to be getting, should have already got but hadn't. "Now you tell your dad I can get up there any time but Saturdays," Doc Loomis said. "I coach on Saturday but I can get up there most any other time. You just tell him to call me."

"I sure will," I said.

"If me or Lenore's not in, we got one of those phone-answering devices," Doc Loomis said.

"I'll tell him," I said.

After a bit I wandered outside on my own. It was amazing how bright the daylight was. My watch said only seven-thirty but the sun was already high up in the sky, bright and glaring as if the clouds had never been there. My car was where I'd left it in the drive, the front door on my father's side still open. I could see houses scattered all around that I hadn't noticed when we'd driven up. A trailer park a quarter mile down the road. An adobe church with a straw roof and a wooden cross. God, what a strange country, I thought; what a strange place to be. Mountains and juniper bushes and red dirt and trailer parks and the bones of Franciscan friars somewhere underfoot. My father's place, as it turned out. His home (whatever that means). The harbor he ended up in, sailing these many years from downstate Illinois, via Rome, London, Hollywood, Dakar, wherever.

I closed the car door and then walked back in the house, past kids in overalls, and Mrs. Loomis, and Doc Loomis on the phone somewhere, past the kitchen, down the corridor, out into the big white shed—the operating room for horses, collies, and old film directors. My father was still on his back asleep. Maria was seated on a little chair at the foot of his table-bed, hands on her lap. She got to her feet when I came near. "Please stay," I said, but she stepped away anyway.

I only wanted to look at him, I don't know what for. Yes I do. I wanted to see if he'd grown back his bulk, his heft, his height—no, it was more than stature. I wanted to see if he'd recovered his full size again. In fact, his face seemed slightly less white than moments ago; not exactly pink but no longer with that ghostly ghastly pallor. His good arm lay outside the sheet. His breathing was definitely more regular.

But he hadn't grown back his size. For a moment, looking down at him, looking down at the shape under the sheet, the outline of legs and knees and torso and so on, I thought: Is *that* all there is of him? Is that . . . all there is of him? My God, what a frightening thing that was to think for the first time; a notion so truly scary in its unexpectedness that without meaning to I reached my hand down to his arm and grasped it, held it hard, held his old skin, could feel the bones beneath the skin. He opened his eyes and looked at me, and then closed them again and slept for another thirty minutes or so until Maria finally prodded him awake ("No more sleep, Sam!") and we took him home.

Time went by in slow motion once again. Originally we'd planned to leave about now—the obligatory trip to Santa Fe and Taos before heading back East—but somehow it didn't seem the right moment for leave-taking, at least not on a junket to Southwestern art galleries and jewelry boutiques. I think I wanted to stay now more than Catherine, who was her old levelheaded self on the surface but seemed jangled underneath, and not so much I felt by what had happened or not happened between her and my father, or by the shooting itself, as by—how shall I say?—the circumstances of the event. "I just can't believe him and Maria!" she said more than once.

"Do you mean because she's dark-skinned?" I finally said, I guess because it was one of the thoughts (if you can properly call it a thought) that had passed through my mind since the Cortez.

"Of course I don't mean because she's dark-skinned!" she said, upset and furious; and then burst into tears. "I didn't even notice she was dark-skinned!" she said as I tried to hug her back into composure.

Maria meanwhile tended my father as a nurse. Trent provided meals, quite adeptly too, though I think nobody had much appetite for food. My father remained in his room, resting, quiet as a mouse, sometimes sitting up in bed with some kind of custard concoction that Maria insisted on fixing for him—like a little old person in his bed I sometimes thought, not quite believing what I was thinking. Now and then I'd look in on him and he'd beam vaguely in my direction. "How are things going, Tom?" he'd say.

"They're fine," I'd say. "Do you want the paper?"

He'd spoon up a morsel of custard. "No, I don't think I want the paper," he'd say.

Once I came in, or was standing in the doorway, while Maria was settling him down for a nap. On his side he was—his right side, his good side; legs bent at the knees. Maria plumped his pillows, rearranged some things on his bedside table. He was lying turned away from me, facing the window though the curtains were partly drawn. His eyes I think were closed, and his hands, or at any rate one of them, like a little kid's, was placed flat between his cheek and the pillow. "Shhh," Maria said sternly, seeing me there. "He sleep." I nodded my head; there really didn't seem to be anything else to say.

He looked just awful when I found him," I was saying. "Like death. The room was so dark I didn't see all the blood at first." I couldn't get that sour little room out of my mind; the way he was sprawled on the bed, the tangle of sheets. Catherine and I were walking together in the afternoon down by the creek, near one of the places where she used to fish. Two small dark trout floated above the bottom of a sandy pool. "Look, they're waiting for you," I said. Part of me I knew wanted time to run backward.

But Catherine was looking elsewhere, out across the fields. "I wonder if Poppa was anything like that," she said as if speaking to herself.

"What do you mean?" I said. But as soon as I said it I thought: Yes, he probably was.

"He was so handsome," she said. "Something more than handsome. Noble. Sometimes he'd be standing there on the bank of our little pond, just staring out. There was never much to look at, not like here. But I always felt he could see beyond what I could see.

Standing there, thinking his noble thoughts like a Roman general. Thinking about *us*, loving *me* . . ."

"I imagine he did," I said.

"I imagine he did sometimes," she said, glancing down at the trout in the water, but with a look on her face that said, No, neither of us thinks like that anymore.

It was a strange time: all that heat and glare and inactivity. Part of me was restless to get back to New York and work and finishing my book and getting on with my life. But part of me—a new part I guess—found it puzzlingly hard to leave my father. To some extent I kept busy answering phone calls, one from the famous Prochnow (who referred to my father as "a class act and a great human being"), several from Newcome, who talked mainly of Prochnow and "problems with the deal" and "salvaging the deal." At one point a car came up the road with an official look to it; police I thought. But it was only the gas company come to check the propane tanks. I asked Maria again about Sánchez. "He gone to El Paso," she said with a shrug. "He better stay there." Late in the afternoon I heard Priscilla in the hallway talking to Catherine.

"How's the old scoundrel?" she said.

"I think he's okay," Catherine said.

"Don't worry, he'll live to be a hundred," Priscilla

said. "I brought him over a cake, I don't know why. He eats too much junk as it is. I probably ought to take it back and feed it to George."

I came down as she was leaving. "Hello, Priscilla," I said.

"Oh, hello, Tom," she said. Mannerly and correct. Dark glasses and a bandanna over her hair.

"I'll walk you to your car," I said.

"You don't have to," she said.

Outside, our shoes crossing the gravel. "Look, I'm sorry," I said.

She stopped beside her car. "But *why*?" she said.

"I thought you were someone else," I said.

"For God's sake, who?" she said.

"It doesn't matter," I said. "But I'm awfully glad it was you instead."

She opened the car door and climbed in. "I can't say that's the most charming compliment a man has ever paid me," she said. "But I suppose it's an answer. Anyway my father always used to say that too much charm in a man was a sign of weakness. Do you agree?"

"I don't know," I said.

"I don't know either," she said. "Well, goodbye, Tom," and she gave me a small smile, and her firm ladylike hand to shake, and off she went.

All of a sudden the house seemed still, oh very still, as if that night had never happened. Odd thoughts and memories kept running through my mind. My father on a lawn somewhere in the sunlight, in a white shirt, his head thrown back, laughing. My mother giving me a watch for my birthday. It came back to me then what he'd said in the car on our way to Doc Loomis—*Fancy seeing you here, Tom*—and I wondered if he'd ever say something like that again to me, and thought probably not, and then thought it didn't matter.

Maria, briefly returned to domestic service, kicked Trent out of the kitchen and made dinner as before. Cold ham and beans. Trent and Catherine and me around the table. Maria marching in and out, brisk and noncommittal. I opened some wine but nobody else wanted any. I offered a glass to Maria. "No wine thank you, Tomás," she said.

For some reason it seemed to get dark early; or perhaps, with my father dozing in his room, there was something hushed and lonely in the air that made it feel like evening. Upstairs I lay on our bed, almost too tired to sleep. Catherine was on the floor doing something with her suitcase, unpacking or repacking it. Finally she too came over to the bed, sat on the edge. I took her in my arms and brought her down beside me, kissed her face and neck. For a moment I thought I could feel tears on her cheeks, but when I looked her eyes were dry.

"I know it's been rough on you," I said.

"Don't talk," she said.

"A lot of bad things went on," I said.

"I don't think they were all bad," she said. "I think I'm very young. I think I have to grow up."

"I have to take care of you better," I said.

"That too," she said.

I could feel her soft against me, tired as if we'd been traveling a long time.

"We could make love," I said.

"We will," she said. "But let's get some sleep first."

We were both in our clothes, too tired to take them off, but I could feel the heaviness of sleep all over me, like a kind of swooning, falling, sinking under the water. I don't know how long we slept, maybe hours or only minutes. It was night outside the window. I kissed Catherine, found her mouth awake, alive. "You promised you'd sleep," she said. "No," I said, stroking, disrobing, touching, kissing—so sweet it all was, and strangely quick, like adolescents. "Too short," I said. "Not too short," she said. We lay together in the darkness for a while. "Say something," she said. "I love you," I said. "Say something more," she said. Without knowing I was going to say it I said, "I wish that had been a baby." She kissed me on the cheek. "There'll be other times," she said.

It felt as if I slept for centuries, but when I woke up it was still dark; maybe not completely dark but predawn dark, five-in-the-morning dark, that tide-rip time between night and day. I pulled the covers over Catherine's bare shoulders, got out of bed, took my shirt and trousers out into the corridor to put them on, went down the stairs. There was a light on in the kitchen but no one there. I wondered how he was sleeping. I wondered if Maria was back in town or in there with him. My father and Maria—there was a thought and a half! I remembered my mother standing in another hallway somewhere fussing with an elaborate silvery evening gown. "Your father always thinks women have to be so *elegant*!" she said with a teenager's pout. I wandered through the living room, looking at it closely in the dusky light, looking at the old rugs and furniture and pottery, conscious that my father and mother had been roughly my age and Catherine's when she wore that silvery dress; conscious for the first time of something I must have known for a long while, that my mother had slept with Charlie Converse; conscious that I would probably never see this place again.

Just then I heard a sound: not quite in the house and not quite outside it. I went through the side door to the porch, stepping into the cool air, feeling the rough planks beneath my feet. Before me were the old wicker chairs, the long, low railing, the slowly lifting darkness above the valley, and in the rocking chair at the far end the figure of my father, seated, facing out, his head hunched forward as if he might be sleeping.

I moved quietly so as not to wake him, then saw the glow of a cigar in one of his hands, also a bottle of some kind of whiskey on the table next to him. I suppose it was thinking about Charlie Converse but I felt a wave of protective feelings I'd never known before—protective of *him*—though what I said was, "Shouldn't you be in bed," addressing him in what I hoped was a proper tone for convalescing patients.

"Fuck bed," said the patient, glancing over at me, no longer I thought quite so little an old man, though his hair was still askew and his beard stubble even more bristly. He wore his blue bathrobe over his bandaged shoulder. "There's some hooch here if you want it," he said.

"No, thanks," I said.

He took a long draw on his cigar, blew out the smoke into the gray dawn. "People say this is the best time of day for thinking," he said, "but sometimes if you start thinking this early you only want to kill yourself." He looked over at me like someone who was beyond arguing such things. "I usually read a little Emerson around now," he said. "Emerson before breakfast. I've read just about everything Emerson ever wrote. Did you know that?"

"I didn't know that," I said.

We sat for a while in silence, listening to the magpies waking up, watching the fields turn from gray to olive green. I took a swig of bourbon and offered him the bottle, holding it near his lips.

"Goddamit, I can do that," he said.

I thought of his naked body lying on that bed in the Cortez. White flesh, white hair.

"I guess I haven't been a very good father to you," I heard him say.

I didn't know what to reply. I thought, you don't have to say that now. "Sometimes I wished you'd been around a whole lot more," I said.

He turned toward me in his chair. "You mean read you fuzzy bedtime stories?"

"I don't know," I said.

"Visit you on parents' day at school?" he said.

"I guess so," I said.

"Christ, I never could stand those smarty-pants schools," he said. "You mean play catch together on Sunday afternoons?"

"Look, you can make fun of anything," I said.

"Who's making fun?" he said. "I remember one spring when we moved from Illinois to Texas. Jesus, there was a lot of snow in Illinois. And wind. Coldest, windiest damn place in the universe. We got down to

Oklahoma I think it was. Nothing but dirt fields and oil pumps. There was a place beside the road where some kind of vines were growing with little white blossoms. I remember we stopped there one afternoon because my ma wasn't feeling too well. She was sitting near the side of the road beside the car. And my dad and I played catch with an old dime-store rubber ball. It was the only time he and I ever played catch but I sure never forgot it." He took another swig from the bottle and started to cough.

"Do you want a slap on the back?" I said.

He glowered at me as the coughing stopped. "I'm the only father you got," he said.

"What's that?" I said.

"I said, goddamit I'm the only father you got."

"I never thought otherwise," I said, which wasn't exactly true. I wondered what he meant by fuzzy bedtime stories, and felt eerily drawn to hugging him though that somehow didn't seem very wise.

"So how come you don't know anything about *me*?" he said.

I couldn't believe my ears. "About *you*?"

"Sure, about me," he said. "How come it's all about *your* schools and parents' days and hard times?"

"I can't believe I'm hearing this," I said.

"What's so hard to believe?" he said, starting to rock himself in the chair, with surprising vigor too, as if he was trying to propel himself off the porch.

"You think I should have been paying more attention to *you*?" I said.

"I didn't say that."

"Yes you did."

"I know what I said. Christ, I remember one time I missed your birthday—"

"One time?" I said.

"For God's sake, you were twelve years old or something," he said. "You weren't no little kid. But boy oh boy your mother gave me hell. And then you'd look at me with those little hurty eyes. Jesus, those little hurty eyes. Did you ever stop to think how many times you remembered *my* birthday?"

"I always remembered your birthday," I said.

"I bet you don't even know when it is," he said.

"November 23," I said. I suddenly found myself on my feet, ready to stalk off the porch.

"Hurty eyes," he repeated, starting to cough again. "You still have hurty eyes."

I heard a window open somewhere in the house, and footsteps across a floor. Down in the field behind the barn two horses trotted into view. I hoped that someone soon would brush my father's hair back into place. "Okay, I have hurty eyes," I said. "Now how about getting back to bed or Maria will have your ass."

My father considered this for a moment, then beckoned me closer. "You know what? I think she wants me to become a Catholic," he said in a hoarse whisper.

"You could do worse," I said.

"It's all incense and mumbo-jumbo," he said.

"Well, they don't take just anyone," I said.

Maria appeared in the doorway, faded flowered tunic, plump brown arms, thick brown legs. She looked at my father, then at me. "You say goodbye to dad," she said to me. It might have been a question, or might not have been.

"I say goodbye," I said, and leaned down and hugged him then, feeling the skin on his face, feeling his rough cheek against mine.

We left Santa Ana later that day, just before noon. The house was quiet; no ringing of telephones; no Trent or Maria in sight. The door to my father's room was closed. I thought, let's knock and say goodbye; but then I thought no, let's leave him be, let's let him sleep, we've said enough goodbyes in both our lives. Bags in the car. A last look around. We were already down the hill, heading past the barn, when Catherine said, "Oh, my God!" I turned my head and slowed the car. There he was —not only there he was, but there he was astride the black horse, still wearing his blue bathrobe, trotting along beside the fence like some old banditti general. I thought, you *heard* me, you heard me thinking you were a little old man, and now, because you're vain and incorrigible, you're going to show off and get yourself killed and make God knows what else amount of mischief if you have the chance. I stopped the car and got out. "You want to come?" I said to Catherine. She seemed to think for a moment. "Sure, I'll come," she said. We walked over to the fence together.

"That's a mighty handsome outfit you're wearing," I said as he came up abreast of us. I was glad to see that at least he was wearing boots instead of bedroom slippers.

"Well, I guess I ain't running for rodeo queen," he said. He shifted a little in the saddle to adjust his bathrobe. "Can you believe what those shitheels are planning to do with *Rio Rigo*?"

"What's that?" I said.

"A fucking TV movie!" he said. "Newcome called. He was pissing in his pants from excitement. Can you believe it? A fucking television movie?"

"Are you going to do it?" Catherine said.

"Of course I'm gonna do it," he said. He spun his horse around in a circle, my only father, arm in a sling, blue bathrobe flapping around his knees. "You want to go for a ride?" he said to me.

"No, I don't want to go for a ride," I said.

"We could go up to the high meadow," he said.

"Maybe jump a few ditches?"

"Maybe so."

"Maybe have a race to the death?"

"We could do that too," he said.

"Look, you take care of yourself," I said, starting to leave.

"Goodbye, Sam," said Catherine.

"Goodbye, gorgeous," he said. Then spun his horse around once more, rose up in the saddle. "Can you imagine?" he said. "Tiny screens and tiny people!" Then waved his one good arm. "Well, hasta la vista!" he said. His farewell address.

Weeks later, back in New York, Catherine said, "So, did you find what you were looking for down there? Did you two become close? Are you two finally friends?"

Friends? I thought. Pals? It was hard to picture the two of us entering any dad-and-son tournaments in the future, or, say, taking a long canoe trip together in the north woods. On the other hand, something of importance clearly had happened in Santa Ana. Was it only that he had lost some height he didn't need, and I had probably gained some height I already had? Was it that we were father and son and doubtless loved each other as best we could? I looked over at Catherine (it was evening and we were riding somewhere in a cab) and it struck me she was more beautiful since we returned, and also in some ways less pretty, less girlish pretty; less of that maiden innocence is what I mean. "In the end I think the person I got closest to was you," I said because it was true.